APHASIOLOGY

Volume 15   Number 7   July 2001

CONTENTS

APHASIOLOGY

SUBSCRIPTION INFORMATION

Subscription rates to Volume 15, 2001 (12 issues) are as follows:

To individuals: UK £304.00; Rest of World $501.00

To institutions: UK £721.00; Rest of World $1190.00

A subscription to the print edition includes free access for any number of concurrent users across a local area network to the online edition, ISSN 1464-5041.
Print subscriptions only are also available to individual members of the British Aphasiology Society (BAS), on application to the Society.

For a complete and up-to-date guide to Taylor & Francis Group's journals and books publishing programmes, visit the Taylor and Francis website: http://www.tandf.co.uk/ . .

Aphasiology (ISSN 0268-7038) is published monthly by Psychology Press, 27 Church Road, Hove, East Sussex BN3 2FA, UK. Annual subscription price US$1190. Air freight and mailing in the USA by Publications Expediting, Inc., 200 Meacham Avenue, Elmont, N.Y. 11003, USA. Periodicals postage paid at Jamaica, N.Y. 11431. US POSTMASTER: send address changes to Aphasiology, Publications Expediting Inc., 200 Meacham, Avenue, Elmont, N.Y. 11003, USA.

Dollar rates apply to subscribers in all countries except the UK and the Republic of Ireland where the pound sterling price applies. All subscriptions are payable in advance and all rates include postage. Journals are sent by air to the USA, Canada, Mexico, India, Japan and Australasia. Subscriptions are entered on an annual basis, *i.e.* from January to December. Payment may be made by sterling cheque, dollar cheque, international money order, National Giro, or credit card (AMEX, VISA, Mastercard).

Orders originating in the following territories should be sent direct to the local distributor.

India Universal Subscription Agency Pvt. Ltd, 101–102 Community Centre, Malviya Nagar Extn, Post Bag No. 8, Saket, New Delhi 110017.
Japan Kinokuniya Company Ltd, Journal Department, PO Box 55, Chitose, Tokyo 156.
USA, Canada and Mexico Psychology Press, a member of the Taylor & Francis Group, 325 Chestnut St, Philadelphia, PA 19106, USA
UK and other territories Taylor & Francis Ltd, Rankine Road, Basingstoke, Hampshire RG24 8PR.

The print edition of this journal is typeset by DP Photosetting, Aylesbury and printed on ANSI conforming acid free paper by the University Press, Cambridge. The online edition of this journal is hosted by Catchword, http://www.catchword.co.uk.

APHASIOLOGY, 2001, *15* (7), 627

Preface

Xavier Seron

Université Catholique de Louvain

There is psychological and neurobiological evidence that number and language processing present some specificities and may dissociate after brain damage. Furthermore, animals and babies seem to be able to discriminate small numerosities in a non-symbolic way. However, one of the specificities of the human species is the development of language and symbolic processes. The acquisition and development of arithmetic is thus bound to the acquisition of language and symbolic notations.

In this Special Issue, the relationship between language and number processing is discussed through the examination of the similarities and divergences of language and number disorders in aphasic subjects, in patients with dementia, and in children with specific acquisition deficits. A separate contribution is also devoted to the rehabilitation of number and calculation deficits in brain-lesioned subjects.

APHASIOLOGY, 2001, *15* (7), 629–633

Introduction

Number and language processing

Xavier Seron

Université catholique de Louvain

At first sight, it may seem strange to present a series of articles on number and calculation disorders in a journal devoted to acquired language disorders. There exist indeed strong arguments suggesting that numbers and calculation constitute a specific cognitive domain that has to be distinguished from language in general. It has been proposed that the ability to recognise and categorise small numerosities of objects or events results from the functioning of a "Number Module" (Butterworth, 1999) or a "Number Sense" (Dehaene, 1997), shared by every member of our species, and which is genetically rooted, present at birth, and sustained by specific brain structures. From a neuropsychological point of view, it is thus expected that arithmetical disorders would follow precise brain lesions affecting the neural structures specifically dedicated to the processing of numerosities and that arithmetical disorders may be dissociated from language disorders. However, in humans, these basic abilities represent only a "starting point" as, due to cultural evolution, we have built a more complex and sophisticated symbolic mathematical knowledge that children have to learn at school. The potentially innate arithmetical competence is thus progressively colonised and probably deeply transformed by the symbolic systems elaborated during recent human history. Where symbolic arithmetic is concerned, language and arithmetic are tightly connected and a large part of our arithmetical abilities implies the use and the manipulation of symbols whether linguistic or numerical. The understanding of human arithmetical competence thus requires—beyond the study of the non-linguistic processes underlying our basic arithmetical abilities—the elucidation of the role played by linguistic processes in the development and the mastery of symbolic arithmetical abilities.

In such a perspective emphasising the relationships between arithmetic and language processes, numbers, just like language, may be considered as a semiotic system (Grewel, 1969; Power & Longuet-Higgins, 1978). A lexicon (the number words and the digits), a syntax (the rules of combination), and a semantic (the numerosities represented) may be defined for the numerical domain, and many activities such as number reading, number writing, or counting may be considered as psycholinguistic activities (Deloche & Seron, 1984a; Seron & Noël, 1992). Numbers, however, differ from other linguistic domains in at least two ways: they can be represented in the written modality by two main different notations (words and digits) and the lexical primitives of the number lexicon are organised in a sequential order.

Address correspondence to: Xavier Seron, Unité NECO Département EXPE, UCL, 10 place Cardinal Mercier, B-1348 Louvain-la-Neuve

http://www.tandf.co.uk/journals/pp/02687038.html DOI:10.1080/02687040143000096

From a linguistic perspective, oral verbal numerals indeed constitute a strictly organised lexicon that has to be learned by rote during childhood and that an educated subject is able to recite in the conventional order as well as in the reverse order (Fuson, 1988). This sequential property is semantically motivated, as in counting activities the recitation of the number names mirrors the increase of the corresponding numerosities. This sequential organisation is, however, not unique to numbers and other parts of the lexicon are also learned in a conventional order (e.g., the letters of the alphabet, the days of the week, the months, or musical notes). At present, we lack sufficient empirical data to establish whether these common properties bear any consequence for the organisation of these lexicons in memory and for the retrieval processes, although some evidence indicates that the access to these ordered lexicons can be simultaneously altered in the case of brain lesions (Cipolotti, Butterworth, & Denes, 1991; Deloche & Seron, 1984b). Numerals (verbal or Arabic) are also organised into sentence-like structures in order to represent any possible numerosity (e.g., "twenty thousand four hundred and sixty five"). These sequences have to obey certain rules that, if not respected, lead to illegal sequences (e.g., "thousand two twenty hundred"). Verbal and Arabic numerals thus *constitute a micro-linguistic domain* that can be, on the one hand, studied *per se* and on the other, studied in relation to more general language processes and structures.

To date, given the paucity of neuropsychological research on this topic, it is not clear whether this micro-linguistic domain is governed by processes and components shared with other language structures or by specific processes. In order to address this question, the examination of the arithmetical abilities of patients presenting various language disorders is, of course, of crucial importance. And, in neuropsychology at least, this question already has a long history because, in 1926, Berger classified as "secondary acalculia" the calculation difficulties resulting from language deficits. Since then, the relationships between language and calculation have regularly been examined in an anatonomical perspective. These earlier studies and the more recent ones are reviewed in this issue by Delazer and Bartha with an emphasis on two main topics: number transcoding and calculation.

With regard to the transcoding of numerals (i.e., going from one numerical code to another), findings in group studies indicate that aphasia is regularly associated with some number-processing disorders. However, one cannot conclude from the co-occurrence of both types of disorders that they result from a common underlying deficit. And, as correctly noted by Delazer and Bartha, some patients with left hemispheric lesions but no aphasia symptoms also present some lexical and syntactic disorders in number processing. The limitations of the group studies do not allow one to test precise hypotheses about the level at which linguistic processes intervene in the transcoding activity and whether these processes do or do not present some specificities. The co-occurrence of arithmetic and language disorders may simply signify that syntactic and lexical processing for numbers and syntactic and lexical mechanisms for language are located in closely adjoining brain areas. Group studies are thus actually not constraining as to the autonomy of the two cognitive domains, but they point to relevant clinical associations of deficits and may lead speech and language therapists to complement their language assessment of aphasic patients with an in-depth examination of number processing and calculation. The single-case studies on number transcoding have mainly been carried out in order to describe and compare rival architectures of the cognitive mechanisms involved in number transcoding. The main controversy concerns whether number-transcoding processes imply access to a semantic representation of the numerosities or whether asemantic transcoding routes also exist. Although the case studies published in the past few years supported the idea of multiple transcoding routes (semantic and non-semantic) (Cipolotti, 1995; Cipolotti & Butterworth, 1995; Cohen & Dehaene, 1995), and even more than a single semantic route (by distinguishing representation of magnitude from numerical encyclopaedic knowledge) (Delazer & Girelli, 1997; Cohen, Dehaene, & Verstichel, 1994), the evidence is not definitively clear, as no double dissociation has been observed as yet (Seron & Noël, 1995). Furthermore, the single-case studies have mainly focused on the numerical transcoding processes and little attention has been paid to the associated linguistic deficits. There is thus a lack of studies comparing, in a systematic way, language and number at different levels of processing (lexical, semantic, syntactic, etc.) (however see Cohen, Verstichel, & Dehaene, 1997).

With regard to calculation, several single-case studies have reported dissociations between language and calculation, but single cases and group studies showing specific associations of deficits have been reported as well (see the review by Delazer and Bartha in this issue). These discrepancies are not necessarily contradictory. One has indeed to distinguish simple arithmetical facts (such as two times three is six) from complex multi-digit mental or written calculation, and to consider that impairments in arithmetic facts retrieval may result from different deficits altering distinct components intervening either at the encoding of the numerals, at the production of the response, or at the level of the retrieval fact in long-term memory (or for complex calculation, in the production or the monitoring of the resolution algorithm). Here too, Delazer and Bartha echo a debate in the literature between those who consider that arithmetical facts are stored in long-term memory in an abstract format (McCloskey, 1992) and those proposing that in order to understand the structures and the processes implied in calculation it is necessary to analyse the different operations separately (Dehaene, 1992; Dehaene & Cohen, 1997). According to this latter view, some arithmetical facts—mainly multiplications and some additions—are taught verbally and systematically at school and are thus stored as verbal associations, whereas subtraction and division would depend on back-up strategies and semantic elaboration (Dehaene & Cohen, 1997). Accordingly, language difficulties with rote verbal memories should be accompanied by difficulties in multiplication and in simple addition, and these operations must generally be impaired together. At present, as pointed out by Delazer and Bartha, the neuropsychological data in favour of the verbal representation thesis are more numerous. Yet, the question is not to find a majority of patients showing the expected profile, but rather to show that all the different patterns of deficits fit a coherent model. The question is not easy to address. Indeed, an important variability in the teaching processes of arithmetical facts might exist, and these differences in the schooling systems might result in variations in the amount of arithmetical facts stored as verbal memories. However, any systematic appeal to variations of schooling types to explain unexpected patterns of dissociations has to be established in an a priori and independent way in order to avoid the circular use of uncontrolled post hoc explanations.

The relationship between language and arithmetic disabilities is also examined in this issue through a developmental perspective by Geary and Hoard. In a broad overview of the literature on developmental arithmetic disabilities, these authors examine three domains of impairment: comprehension of numbers, counting, and calculation. They critically analyse the various cognitive components that have been proposed to cause these different deficits, as well as the associated neural damage. In a last section, they discuss some potential factors that may underline the regular co-morbidity observed in arithmetic disabilities and dyslexia. They correctly underline that the difficulty in processing the sounds of language, considered by many as the core deficit for most dyslexics, could also result in delays or difficulties in the acquisition of verbal counting, which in turn may lead to an impairment in the elaboration and retrieval of arithmetical facts. The authors also contrast arithmetic disabilities due to procedural deficits, which, tentatively, could be linked to neurodevelopmental disabilities in the prefrontal cortex, with arithmetic disabilities consisting of difficulties in fact-access that they propose result from neurodevelopmental abnormalities in the posterior regions of the left hemisphere. These group studies pointing to regular patterns· of association and dissociation of developmental deficits are clinically relevant and raise interesting theoretical questions. They surely indicate that one has to distinguish different kinds of arithmetic developmental disabilities and that those present together with language disorders may be of another nature than those appearing in isolation or in co-occurrence with other neuropsychological impairments. My feeling is that developmental group studies should here be complemented by single-case studies conducted in a truly longitudinal perspective.

In a subsequent paper, Girelli and Delazer examine the fate of numerical abilities in dementia. Although the studies devoted to this topic are not numerous, the occurrence of dyscalculia in the early stages of Alzheimer's disease (AD) has often been noticed. The authors' thorough examination of the literature indicates that arithmetic difficulties vary greatly across individuals, being either highly selective or more extended to all aspects of numerical abilities. Some single-case studies have also shown that one can find in AD the same sort of selective deficit observed after focal lesions, as well as the selective preservation of some calculation abilities due either to an exceptional pre-morbid expertise or to the intrinsic variability of the brain damage. Finally, the authors also underline the existence of some specific difficulties in written transcoding tasks in AD, consisting in the intrusion of the Arabic notation code into the verbal code or the reverse. These transcoding deficits, which up to now have not been observed in patients with focal lesions and which occur very rarely in normal elderly subjects, may well constitute an impairment specific to the determined condition.

Finally, in the last contribution, Girelli and Seron present the rare studies that have been devoted to the rehabilitation of calculation and number-processing deficits. This aspect has not yet been fully developed and, at present, therapeutic attempts have been limited to three domains: number transcoding, arithmetical facts retrieval, and problem solving. In the domain of number transcoding and retrieval of arithmetic facts, the rehabilitation has been reconstructive in nature. The idea underlying such a re-establishment rationale is that the numerical domain and basic arithmetic are relatively limited in extension and, as a consequence, the objective of re-teaching such a limited knowledge has been considered as a not-too-demanding task. Although modest in extension, most of the rehabilitation programmes have resulted in some success and, in the transcoding domain, they have already been applied to dyscalculic children. In the near future, one may expect the development of compensatory rehabilitation strategies in this domain, at least if the reconstructive strategies appear inefficient or too time-consuming.

Finally, the main objective of this special issue will have been fully attained if, after reading these synthetic articles, speech and language therapists really consider the number domain as a pertinent area of investigation for diagnosis, theoretical work, and rehabilitation. Too often in clinical practice, the numerical domain is only considered in the language evaluation batteries under the heading of "automatic speech": the patient's competence is simply evaluated through the recitation of the conventional number word sequences. It is patently evident that the domain of cognitive arithmetic requires more attention: the use of numbers is of critical importance in many daily life activities, and speech and language therapists should be greatly concerned, as at least some of the arithmetical difficulties resulting from brain damage are the consequence of associated language disorders.

REFERENCES

Butterworth, B. (1999). *The mathematical brain*. London: MacMillan.

Cipolotti, L. (1995). Multiple routes for reading words, why not numbers? Evidence from a case of Arabic numeral dyslexia. *Cognitive Neuropsychology, 12*, 313–342.

Cipolotti, L., & Butterworth, B. (1995). Toward a multiroute model of number processing: Impaired number transcoding with preserved calculation skills. *Journal of Experimental Psychology: General, 124*, 375–390.

Cipolotti, L., Butterworth, B., & Denes, G. (1991). A specific deficit for numbers in a case of dense acalculia. *Brain, 114*, 2619–2637.

Cohen, L., & Dehaene, S. (1995). Number processing in pure alexia: The effect of hemispheric asymmetries and tasks demands. *Neurocase, 1*, 121–137.

Cohen, L., Dehaene, S., & Verstichel, P. (1994). Number words and number non-words: A case of deep dyslexia extending to arabic numerals. *Brain, 117*, 267–279.

Cohen, L., Verstichel, P., & Dehaene, S. (1997). Neologistic jargon sparing numbers: A category-specific phonological impairment. *Cognitive Neuropsychology, 14*, 1029–1061.

Dehaene, S. (1992). Varieties of numerical abilities, *Cognition, 44*, 1–42.

Dehaene, S. (1997). *The number sense: How the mind creates mathematics*. New York: Oxford University Press.

Dehaene, S., & Cohen, L. (1997). Cerebral pathways for calculation: Double dissociation between rote verbal and quantitative knowledge of arithmetic. *Cortex, 33*, 219–250.

Delazer, M., & Girelli, L. (1997). When Alfa Romeo facilitates 164: Semantic effects in verbal number production. *Neurocase, 3*, 461–475.

Deloche, G., & Seron, X. (1984a). Some linguistic components of acaleulia. In F.C. Rose (Ed.), *Advances in neurology, Vol. 42: Progress in aphasiology* (pp. 215–222). New York: Raven Press.

Deloche, G., & Seron, X. (1984b). Semantic errors reconsidered in the procedural light of stack concepts. *Brain and Language, 21*, 59–71.

Fuson, K.C. (1988). *Children's counting and concepts of number*. New York: Springer-Verlag.

Grewel, F. (1969). The acalculias. In P.J. Vinken & G. Bruyn (Eds.), *Handbook of clinical neurology, Vol. 3*. Amsterdam: North Holland.

McCloskey, M. (1992). Cognitive mechanisms in numerical processing: Evidence from acquired dyscalculia. *Cognition, 44*, 107–157.

Power, R.J.D., & Longuet-Higgins, J.C. (1978). Learning to count: A computational model of language acquisition. *Proceedings of the Royal Society of London, 200*, 391–417.

Seron, X., & Noël, M.P. (1992). Language and numerical disorders, a neuropsychological approach. In J. Alegria, D., Holendar, J. Morais, & M. Radeau, (Eds.), *Analytical approaches to human cognition* (pp. 291–309). Amsterdam: Elsevier Publishing Company.

Seron, X., & Noël, M.P. (1995). Transcoding numbers from the arabic code to the verbal one or vice versa: How many routes? *Mathematical Cognition, 1*, 215–243.

APHASIOLOGY, 2001, *15* (7), 635–647

Numerical and arithmetical deficits in learning-disabled children: Relation to dyscalculia and dyslexia

David C. Geary and Mary K. Hoard

University of Missouri, USA

Cognitive research on the number, counting, and arithmetic competencies of children with a learning disability in arithmetic (AD) is reviewed, and similarities between the associated deficits of AD children and the deficits of individuals afflicted with dyscalculia are highlighted. It is concluded that the defining features of AD and most dyscalculias are difficulties with the procedural features associated with the solving of complex arithmetic problems and difficulties in remembering basic arithmetic facts. The procedural deficits and one form of retrieval deficit appear to be associated with functioning of the prefrontal cortex, while a second form of retrieval deficit appears to be associated with the functioning of the left parieto-occipito-temporal areas and several subcortical structures. The review ends with a discussion of the potential relation between this second form of retrieval deficit and dyslexia.

Acquired and developmental dyscalculia refer to deficits in the processing of numerical and arithmetical information that are associated with overt brain injury or presumed neurodevelopmental abnormalities, respectively. Research in this area has yielded a wealth of insights into the architecture of the cognitive and associated neural systems that support basic quantitative abilities and has provided insights into the core deficits of dyscalculia (Dehaene & Cohen, 1995, 1997; Girelli, Delazer, Semenza, & Denes, 1996; Hittmair-Delazer, Sailer, & Benke, 1995; Levin et al., 1996; McCloskey, Caramazza, & Basili, 1985; McCloskey & Macaruso, 1995; Pesenti, Seron, & Van der Linden, 1994; Semenza, Miceli, & Girelli, 1997; Temple, 1989, 1991). Although the two domains of study are not often linked, the cognitive deficits of children with a learning disability in arithmetic (AD) are very similar to those associated with acquired and developmental dyscalculia (Geary, 1993). The goals here are to provide a review of the numerical and arithmetical deficits of AD children, to illustrate empirical and conceptual links between these deficits and those associated with dyscalculia, and, finally, to explore the relation between AD and dyslexia.

Large-scale studies suggest that AD children constitute between 6% and 7% of the school-age population (Badian, 1983; Gross-Tsur, Manor, & Shalev, 1996; Kosc, 1974), and indicate that the number of children affected by AD is comparable to the number of children affected by reading disabilities (RD), or dyslexia. In fact, AD and dyslexia are comorbid in many children (Ackerman & Dykman, 1995). Cognitive studies of AD

Address correspondence to: David C. Geary, Department of Psychology, 210 McAlester Hall, University of Missouri, Columbia, MO 65211-2500, USA. Email: GearyD@missouri.edu

http://www.tandf.co.uk/journals/pp/02687038.html   DOI:10.1080/02687040143000113

children have, to a large degree, been based on the conceptual models and experimental measures used to study the development of number, counting, and arithmetic competencies in normal children (Geary, 1990, 1994; Jordan, Levine, & Huttenlocher, 1995; Siegler, 1996; Siegler & Shrager, 1984). The use of this approach has provided theoretical coherence to the study of AD children and has enabled their deficits to be understood within the broader context of normal numerical and arithmetical development. The sections that follow provide a brief overview of normal development in the areas of number, counting, and arithmetic, along with discussion of any deficits found with AD children and related deficits in dyscalculia. The final section presents discussion of the potential relation between AD and dyslexia.

NUMERICAL AND ARITHMETICAL COGNITION

Number

Models of children's ability to understand and produce numbers have been informed by research on normally developing children and by research on disruptions in the ability to process and understand the meaning of numbers following brain injury (Fuson, 1988; McCloskey et al., 1985; McCloskey & Macaruso, 1995; Seron & Fayol, 1994). Across these areas, number production and comprehension are understood to require the ability to process verbal (e.g., "three hundred forty two") and Arabic representations of numbers (e.g., "342"), and to transcode, or translate, numbers from one representation to another (e.g., "three hundred forty two" to "342"; Dehaene, 1992; McCloskey, 1992). Number comprehension also requires that the individual understand the meaning of the processed numbers. Early in development, number comprehension is evidenced when, among other things, children associate number names and Arabic representations with the associated quantities and understand ordinal relations among these quantities (e.g., that $3 > 2$; Fuson, 1988; Geary, 1994). Later, children are expected to understand more complex relations among numbers; for instance, that the 3 in 342 represents 3 sets of 100s.

Although not typical (e.g., Semenza et al., 1997; Temple, 1991), disruptions in the ability to understand, produce, or transcode numbers are sometimes evident with acquired (McCloskey, Sokol, & Goodman, 1986) and developmental (Temple, 1989) dyscalculia. The associated deficits can involve difficulties in lexical access—stating a number word that is numerically close to the correct number word (e.g., stating "nine" when presented with "7", or twenty-two when presented with "28")—or in number syntax. Syntax refers to the base-10 structure of the Arabic number system; that is, that the values of the integers in different columns of complex numbers, such as 342, differ by a factor of ten. An understanding of the meaning of the structure of the associated sequence of number words is equally important, such as "three hundred fifty six" (e.g., "six" refers to 6 units, not 6 tens). Disruptions in the syntactic structure of number processing might be reflected, for instance, in errors in transcoding verbal to Arabic representations, such as transcoding "eighty four" as "804" (McCloskey et al., 1986; Seron & Fayol, 1994). Difficulties in lexical access and number syntax are often associated with damage to the left hemisphere, while deficits in number comprehension are sometimes associated with damage to the inferior parietal cortex of either hemisphere (Dehaene & Cohen, 1995, 1997; see also Temple & Posner, 1998).

Number production and comprehension skills have not been as systematically studied in AD children as they have in individuals afflicted with dyscalculia. The few studies that have been conducted suggest that the cognitive and neural systems that support number production and comprehension are generally intact in AD children, at least for the processing of simple numbers (e.g., 6 9; Badian, 1983; Geary, 1993; Gross-Tsur et al., 1996; Russell & Ginsburg, 1984). Nonetheless, some first-grade AD children do have difficulties in identifying and producing numbers greater than 10 and in determining which of two consecutive Arabic numbers, such as 8 9, represents the larger quantity (Geary, Hoard, & Hamson, 1999). These difficulties appear to be restricted to first grade (Geary, Hamson, & Hoard, 2000). Nonetheless, it is not currently known whether AD children have deficits in the ability to comprehend and produce more complex numbers, such as 342, above and beyond the difficulties found in normal children (Seron & Fayol, 1994).

Counting

The study of children's counting competencies has largely focused on their understanding of the underlying concepts rather than the ability to count in a rote fashion. Children's counting knowledge appears to emerge from a combination of inherent and experiential factors (Briars & Siegler, 1984; Geary, 1995; Gelman & Gallistel, 1978). Early inherent constraints can be represented by Gelman and Gallistel's five implicit principles; one–one correspondence (one and only one word tag, e.g., "one", "two", is assigned to each counted object); the stable order principle (the order of the word tags must be invariant across counted sets); the cardinality principle (the value of the final word tag represents the quantity of items in the counted set); the abstraction principle (objects of any kind can be collected together and counted); and, the order-irrelevance principle (items within a given set can be tagged in any sequence). The principles of one–one correspondence, stable order, and cardinality define the "how to count" rules, which, in turn, provide constraints on the nature of preschool children's counting behaviour and provide the skeletal structure for children's emerging knowledge of counting.

Children also appear to make inductions about the basic characteristics of counting, by observing standard counting behaviour (Briars & Siegler, 1984; Fuson, 1988). This induced knowledge reflects both essential features of counting, such as those identified by Gelman and Gallistel (1978), and unessential features of counting (Briars & Siegler, 1984). These unessential features include standard direction (counting starts at one of the end points of an array of objects); adjacency (a consecutive count of contiguous objects); pointing (counted objects are typically pointed at but only once); and, start at an end (counting proceeds from left to right). By 5 years of age, many children know the essential features of counting but also believe that adjacency and start at an end are essential features of counting. The latter beliefs indicate that young children's counting knowledge is immature and influenced by the observation of counting procedures.

Individuals with acquired or developmental dyscalculia are generally able to count arrays of objects and recite the correct sequence of number words during the act of counting (e.g., counting from 1 to 20; Hittmair-Delazer et al., 1995; Pesenti et al., 1994; Temple, 1989). However, individuals with damage to the right hemisphere sometimes show difficulties with the procedural component of counting; specifically, difficulties in systematically pointing to successive objects as they are enumerated (Seron et al., 1991). Individuals with damage to the left hemisphere sometimes have difficulties in producing number names. Even with such difficulties, most of these individuals appear to understand many of the basic principles, such as cardinality, identified by Gelman and Gallistel (1978; Seron et al., 1991).

Similarly, Geary and his colleagues found that first-grade children with comorbid AD and dyslexia understand most of the essential features of counting, such as stable order and cardinality (Geary, Bow-Thomas, & Yao, 1992). However, these children consistently made errors on tasks that assess adjacency and order-irrelevance. A more recent study confirmed this finding (Geary et al., 1999; Geary et al., 2000). Using IQ as a covariate, Geary et al. showed that children with comorbid AD and dyslexia and AD-only children made similar errors on order-irrelevance or adjacency tasks in both first and second grade. In contrast, dyslexic children with average or better mathematics achievement scores did not differ from normal children on the associated tasks. The results suggests that many young AD children, regardless of their reading or IQ status, do not understand the order-irrelevance principle, or, from Briars and Siegler's (1984) perspective, they believe that adjacency is an essential feature of counting. The overall pattern suggests that young AD children, as a group, understand counting as a rote, mechanical activity, although it is not currently known whether this immature counting knowledge extends beyond second grade.

In these same studies, it was found that some AD children have difficulties on counting tasks that involve detecting double-counting errors, although the magnitude of this effect is not as large as that found for the order-irrelevance task (Geary et al., 1992; Geary et al., 1999). Specifically, many of these children fail to detect errors that involve double counting the first, but not the last, item (e.g., pointing at the first item twice in succession and stating "one, two"). Detection of an error when the item is double counted suggests that these AD children understand the one–one correspondence principle. At same time, the failure to note that the double counting of the first item is an error suggests that many of these children cannot retain an "error notation" in working memory while monitoring the counting process (see also Hitch & McAuley, 1991; Hoard, Geary, & Hamson, 1999).

Arithmetic

The cognitive competencies associated with the solving of simple arithmetic problems and the development of these competencies have been extensively studied during the past 25 years (e.g., Ashcraft, 1982, 1995; Ashcraft & Fierman, 1982; Carpenter & Moser, 1984; Geary, 1994; Groen & Parkman, 1972; Seigler, 1996; Siegler & Shrager, 1984). Developmental and schooling-based improvements in basic arithmetical competencies are reflected in changes in the distribution of procedures, or strategies, used in problem solving and in advances in children's conceptual understanding of arithmetic and related domains, such as counting (Geary, 1994).

When first learning to solve simple arithmetic problems, such as $5 + 3$, children rely on their knowledge of counting and counting procedures; that is, children typically count the addends to solve such problems. These counting procedures are sometimes executed with the aid of fingers—the finger counting strategy—and sometimes without them—the verbal counting strategy (Siegler & Shrager, 1984). The two most commonly used counting procedures, whether children use their fingers or not, are termed min (or counting-on) and sum (or counting-all; Fuson, 1982; Groen & Parkman, 1972). The min procedure involves stating the larger-valued addend and then counting a number of times equal to the value of the smaller addend, such as counting 5, 6, 7, 8 to solve $5 + 3$. The sum procedure involves counting both addends starting from 1. Occasionally, children will state the value of the smaller addend and then count the larger addend, which is termed the max procedure. The development of procedural competencies is reflected in a gradual shift from heavy reliance on the sum and max procedures to frequent use of min counting (Siegler, 1987). This shift is related, in part, to improvements in the children's conceptual understanding of counting (Geary et al., 1992).

Simple arithmetic problems are also solved by means of memory-based processes, specifically direct retrieval of arithmetic facts, decomposition, and fingers. With direct retrieval, children state an answer that is associated in long-term memory with the presented problem, such as stating ''/eyt/'' (i.e., eight) when asked to solve $5 + 3$. Decomposition involves reconstructing the answer based on the retrieval of a partial sum. For instance, the problem $6 + 7$ might be solved by retrieving the answer to $6 + 6$ (i.e., 12) and then adding 1 to this partial sum. With the fingers strategy, children uplift a number of fingers corresponding to the addends and then state an answer without counting their fingers. The uplifted fingers appear to prompt retrieval of the answer.

The use of memory-based processes appears to follow from the use of counting procedures; that is, the frequent use of counting procedures eventually leads to the formation of associations between problems and the answers generated by means of counting. The problem/answer associations, in turn, provide the basis for direct retrieval, decomposition, and fingers (see Siegler, 1996, for a more thorough discussion). However, the use of retrieval-based processes is moderated by a confidence criterion. The confidence criterion represents an internal standard against which the child gauges confidence in the correctness of the retrieved answer. Children with a rigorous confidence criterion only state answers that they are certain are correct, whereas children with a lenient criterion state any retrieved answer, correct or not (Siegler, 1988).

These developmental findings and the accompanying conceptual models have provided a useful framework for the study of AD children's difficulties in learning basic arithmetic. Studies conducted in the United States, Europe, and Israel have revealed consistent differences in the procedural and memory-based processes used by normal and AD children to solve simple arithmetic problems (e.g., Barrouillet, Fayol, & Lathulière, 1997; Geary, 1990; Geary & Brown, 1991; Geary, Brown, & Samaranayake, 1991; Gross-Tsur et al., 1996; Jordan & Montani, 1997; Ostad, 1997, 1998; Räsänen & Ahonen, 1995; Svenson & Broquist, 1975). In fact, the procedural and memory-based deficits that are common in AD children are also common in acquired and developmental dyscalculia (e.g., Geary, 1993; Pesenti et al., 1994; Temple, 1991). Double dissociations between procedural and memory-based processes are often found with dyscalculia (Dehaene & Cohen, 1997; Semenza et al., 1997; Temple, 1991) and are sometimes found in AD children (Geary et al., 1991; Jordan & Montani, 1997). For these reasons, procedural and memory-based deficits are presented in separate sections here.

Procedural deficits.   Much of the research on AD children has focused on their use of counting procedures to solve arithmetic problems. When using these procedures, young AD children commit more errors than do their normal peers (Geary, 1990; Jordan et al., 1995; Jordan & Montani, 1997). The errors result as these children miscount or lose track of the counting process. As a group, AD children also rely on finger counting and use the sum procedure more frequently than do normal children. Although it is not yet certain, their use of finger counting appears to be a working memory aid, in that it helps these children to keep track of the counting process. Their delayed use of min counting appears to be related, in part, to their immature counting knowledge (Geary, 1990; Geary et al., 1992). However, many, but not all, of these children show more normal procedural skills by the middle of the elementary school years (Geary et al., 1991; Geary & Brown, 1991; Geary et al., 1999; Jordan & Montani, 1997). For these children, their error-prone use of immature procedures represents a developmental delay rather than a long-term cognitive deficit (Geary & Brown, 1991; Russell & Ginsburg, 1984).

In an assessment of skill at solving more complex arithmetic problems, such as 45×12 or $126 + 537$, Russell and Ginsburg (1984) found that fourth-grade AD children committed more errors than did their IQ-matched normal peers. These errors involved the misalignment of numbers while writing down partial answers or errors while carrying or borrowing from one column to the next. At the same time, these AD children appeared to understand the base-10 system as well as did the normal children, and thus the errors could not be attributed to a poor conceptual understanding of the structure of the problems. Rather, many of the errors appeared to result from difficulties in monitoring the sequence of problem-solving steps and from poor skills in detecting and then self-correcting errors. Similarly, Geary et al. (1992) found that many first-grade children with comorbid AD and dyslexia did not detect and self-correct counting errors as readily as did their normal peers. Although it is not certain, it appears that for many AD children these deficits persist at least through the elementary school years and probably longer (Geary, 1994).

Difficulties in the solving of complex arithmetic problems are also common with acquired and developmental dyscalculia (Semenza et al., 1997; Temple, 1991). As an example, in an extensive assessment of the counting, number, and arithmetic competencies of a 17-year-old (MM) with severe congenital damage to the right frontal and parietal cortices, Semenza and his colleagues reported deficits very similar to those found by Russell and Ginsburg (1984) with AD children. Basic number and counting skills were intact, as was the ability to retrieval basic facts (such as 8 for $5 + 3$) from memory. However, MM had difficulty solving complex division and multiplication problems, such as 32×67. Of particular difficulty was tracking the sequence of partial products. Once the first step was completed (2×7), difficulties in placing the partial product (4) in the correct position and carrying to the next column were evident. Thus, the primary deficit of MM appeared to involve difficulties in sequencing the order of operations and in monitoring the problem-solving process, as is often found with damage to the frontal cortex (Luria, 1980). Temple (1991) reported a similar pattern of procedural difficulties for an individual with neurodevelopmental abnormalities in the right-frontal cortex.

Memory retrieval deficits.   Many AD children do not show the shift from procedural-based problem solving to memory-based problem solving that is commonly found in normal children (Geary, Widaman, Little, & Cormier, 1987; Ostad, 1997), suggesting difficulties in storing or accessing arithmetic facts in or from long-term memory. Indeed, disrupted memory-based processes are consistently found with comparisons of AD and normal children (Barrouillet et al., 1997; Bull & Johnston, 1997; Garnett & Fleischner, 1983; Geary, 1993; Geary & Brown, 1991; Geary et al., 1987; Jordan & Montani, 1997; Ostad, 1997, 1998) and are very frequently a feature of dyscalculia (Dehaene & Cohen, 1991, 1997; Hittmair-Delazer et al., 1995; Levin et al., 1996; Pesenti et al., 1994). Disruptions in the ability to retrieve basic facts from long-term memory might, in fact, be considered the defining feature of AD and most, but not all, cases of dyscalculia (Geary, 1993). However, most of these individuals can retrieve some facts, and disruptions in the ability to retrieve facts associated with one operation (e.g., multiplication) are sometimes found with intact retrieval of facts associated with another operation, at least with dyscalculia (e.g., subtraction; Pesenti et al., 1994).

When they retrieve arithmetic facts from long-term memory, AD children commit many more errors than do their normal peers, and show error and reaction time (RT) patterns that often differ from the patterns found with younger, normal children (Geary, 1993; Geary et al., 2000). The RT patterns are similar to the patterns found with children who have suffered from an early (before age 8 years) lesion to the left-hemisphere or associated subcortical regions (Ashcraft, Yamashita, & Aram, 1992). Although this pattern does not necessarily indicate that AD children have suffered from some form of overt brain injury, it does suggest that the memory-based deficits of many AD children may reflect the same mechanisms underlying the retrieval deficits associated with dyscalculia (Geary, 1993; Rourke, 1993).

However, the cognitive and neural mechanisms underlying these deficits are not completely understood. At this point, it appears that there might be two different forms of retrieval deficit, each reflecting a disruption to different cognitive and neural systems (Barrouillet et al., 1997; Dehaene & Cohen, 1997; Geary et al., 2000). The work of Dehaene and his colleagues suggests that the retrieval of arithmetic facts is supported by a system of neural structures, including the left basal ganglia, thalamus, and the left parieto-occipito-temporal areas (Dehaene & Cohen, 1995, 1997). Damage to either the subcortical or cortical structures in this network is associated with difficulties in accessing previously known arithmetic facts (Dehaene & Cohen, 1991, 1997). Cognitive studies of AD children also support the view that their retrieval deficits are due, in part, to difficulties in accessing facts from long-term memory (Geary, 1993). However, it is not currently known if these deficits are associated with damage to or neurodevelopmental abnormalities in the regions identified by Dehaene and Cohen (1995, 1997).

More recent studies of AD children suggest a second form of retrieval deficit; specifically, disruptions in the retrieval process due to difficulties in inhibiting the retrieval of irrelevant associations. This form of retrieval deficit was first discovered by Barrouillet et al. (1997), based on the memory model of Conway and Engle (1994), and was recently confirmed by Geary and his colleagues (Geary et al., 2000; see also Koontz & Berch, 1996). In the latter study, children with comorbid AD and dyslexia, AD only, and dyslexia only were compared to their normal peers on an array of number, counting, arithmetic, and memory tasks in first and second grade. One of the arithmetic tasks administered in second grade required the children to only use retrieval—the children were instructed not to use counting strategies—to solve simple addition problems. Children in all of the learning-disability groups committed more retrieval errors than did their normal peers, even after controlling for IQ. The most common of these errors was a counting string associate of one of the addends. For instance, common retrieval errors for the problem $6 + 2$ were 7 and 3, the numbers following 6 and 2, respectively, in the counting sequence.

The pattern in this study and that of Barrouillet et al. (1997) is in keeping with Conway and Engle's (1994) position that individual differences in working memory and retrieval efficiency are related, in part, to inefficient inhibition of irrelevant associations. In this model, the presentation of a to-be-solved problem results in the activation of relevant information in working memory, including problem features—such as the addends in a simple addition problem—and information associated with these features. Problem solving is efficient when irrelevant associations are inhibited and prevented from entering working memory. Insufficient inhibition results in activation of irrelevant information, which functionally lowers working memory capacity. In this view, AD children make retrieval errors, in part, because they cannot inhibit irrelevant associations from entering working memory. Once in working memory these associations either suppress or compete with the correct association for expression. Whatever the cognitive mechanism, these results suggest that the retrieval deficits of some AD children result either from delayed development of the prefrontal cortex or from neurodevelopmental abnormalities in these regions (Bull, Johnston, & Roy, 1999; Luria, 1980; Welsh & Pennington, 1988).

Summary

Most AD children and most individuals afflicted with dyscalculia perform as well as their normal peers on tasks of number production and comprehension. When deficits are found, they often involve difficulties in accessing the appropriate number name, difficulties with the syntax of complex numbers, or in accessing the quantities associated with verbal or Arabic number representations. The former deficits are often associated with lesions to the left hemisphere, while the latter is often associated with damage to the inferior parietal cortices of either hemisphere (Dehaene & Cohen, 1997; Geary, 1993; Seron et al., 1991). At this point, it is not known if these same neural systems are involved in the number comprehension and production difficulties of some young AD children.

For the most part, AD children and individuals afflicted with dyscalculia understand the basic counting principles identified by Gelman and Gallistel (1978; Geary et al., 1992; Seron et al., 1991). Difficulties in the procedural components of counting—difficulties in systematically pointing to objects as they are counted—are sometimes found with lesions to the right hemisphere. Difficulties in retrieving number words during the act of counting are associated with lesions to the left hemisphere (Seron et al., 1991). Although AD children understand the basic principles of counting, they also believe that counting *must* involve counting and tagging with a number word each object in succession; that is, skipping around during the count is not acceptable (Geary et al., 1992; Geary et al., 2000). This finding suggests that many of these children view counting as a rote, mechanical activity, which, in turn, appears to contribute to their delayed use of min counting; because the task that is sensitive to this knowledge has not been administered in the dyscalculia studies, it is not currently known if the same pattern will emerge with these individuals.

All in all, difficulties in solving simple and complex arithmetic problems are the defining feature of dyscalculia and AD (Geary, 1993; Temple, 1991). These difficulties are subsumed under procedural and retrieval deficits. For both AD children and individuals afflicted with dyscalculia, procedural deficits are typically evident during the solving of complex arithmetic problems, such as $362 + 973$, but do not appear to be due to a poor understanding of the associated concepts (e.g., the base-10 system; Semenza et al., 1997). Rather, errors during the solving of these problems appear to reflect difficulties in sequencing the associated component processes (e.g., keeping track of partial sums) and in detecting and self-correcting errors (Russell & Ginsburg, 1984; Semenza et al., 1997; Temple, 1991). With dyscalculia, these difficulties are typically associated with damage to the prefrontal cortex (Luria, 1980; Semenza et al., 1997; Temple, 1991). However, it is not currently known if AD children have neurodevelopmental abnormalities or delayed maturation of the prefrontal cortex, although either of these is a distinct possibility (Bull et al., 1999).

In young AD children, procedural errors are often found during the solving of simple arithmetic problems. When using counting procedures to solve these problems, AD children often miscount, lose track of the counting process, and use developmentally immature procedures (e.g., sum counting on their fingers; Geary, 1990). The latter appears to be related to their rather rigid understanding of counting (Geary et al., 1992). For most of these children, these procedural difficulties appear to reflect a developmental delay rather than a cognitive deficit (Geary et al., 1991) and, given this, it is not likely that the same mechanisms are involved in these procedural difficulties and those associated with the solving of more complex problems.

Difficulties in remembering arithmetic facts and a high frequency of errors and unusual RT patterns for those facts that are retrieved are common in AD and dyscalculia (Dehaene & Cohen, 1991; Garnett & Fleischner, 1983; Geary, 1993; Temple, 1991). These memory deficits appear to take two forms, one involving difficulties in the accessing of facts from long-term memory and the other involving irrelevant associations interfering with the retrieval process (Barrouillet et al., 1997; Geary, 1993). The first of these deficits appears to be associated with damage to or neurodevelopmental abnormalities in the left parieto-occipito-temporal areas or associated subcortical structures, specifically the basal ganglia and thalamus (Dehaene & Cohen, 1995, 1997). The second form of retrieval deficit is most likely related to the functioning of the prefrontal cortex. However, a definitive association between the integrity of these neural areas and AD has yet to be established.

ARITHMETIC DISABILITIES AND DYSLEXIA

For most dyslexic readers, the core deficit involves the neural and cognitive systems that support the processing of language sounds or phonemes (e.g., Morris et al., 1998). This basic deficit is manifested as a lack of phonetic awareness, as well as difficulties in segmenting language sounds and in retrieving words from long-term memory (Denckla & Rudel, 1976; Shankweiler et al., 1995). These difficulties are moderately heritable and are often associated with neurodevelopmental abnormalities in the cortical and subcortical systems that support language processing (Hynd & Semrud-Clikeman, 1989; Olson et al., 1989). The issue here is whether there is a relation between difficulties in processing language sounds and the comorbidity of AD and dyslexia (Rourke & Finlayson, 1978).

Theoretically, difficulties in the processing of language sounds could also result in AD, specifically difficulties in accessing arithmetic facts from long-term memory. As described earlier, the long-term memory representations between arithmetic problems and the associated answers appear to form as children use counting procedures to solve the problems (Siegler & Shrager, 1984). In other words, the repeated use of counting to solve problems, such as $5+3$, eventually leads to the formation of an association between the problem and the answers generated by means of counting. After many counts, the presentation of the problem leads to the automatic retrieval of the associated answer. Because counting involves the articulation of number words—that is, the use of the basic phonetic and language systems—the associations in long-term memory between problems and answers should be represented, at least in part, in the same phonetic and semantic memory systems that support word processing and word retrieval. Any neurodevelopmental disruptions in the functioning of these systems might then place the individual at risk for dyslexia and for difficulties in the arithmetical processes that are supported by the same systems, such as fact retrieval.

On the basis of these theoretical considerations and on the comorbidity of AD and dyslexia, Geary (1993, p. 356) argued that these disorders co-occur because of a common underlying neuropsychological deficit, perhaps involving the posterior regions of the left hemisphere. At the cognitive level, this deficit manifests itself as difficulties in the representation and retrieval of semantic information from long-term memory. This would include fact retrieval problems in simple arithmetic and, for instance, word-recognition and phonological-awareness difficulties in reading.

Although it now appears that fact-retrieval deficits are more varied than originally believed, recent results confirm that children with comorbid AD and dyslexia are slower at accessing number and word names from long-term memory than are their normal peers and show arithmetic fact-retrieval deficits (Geary et al., 2000). Based on the work of Dehaene and Cohen (1995, 1997) and others (Hynd & Semrud-Clikeman, 1989), it appears that difficulties in accessing arithmetic facts and words from long-term memory might also result from damage to or neurodevelopmental abnormalities in subcortical regions, particularly the basal ganglia and perhaps the thalamus. It still remains to be demonstrated, however, that the neural systems underlying the word retrieval difficulties associated with dyslexia and the fact-retrieval problems associated with AD are one and the same.

CONCLUSION

Acquired and developmental dyscalculia share many features with one another and with AD. The most common of these features are difficulties with the procedural components of solving complex, and sometimes simple, arithmetic problems and with remembering basic arithmetic facts. The procedural deficits as well as one form of retrieval deficit appear to result from damage to or neurodevelopmental abnormalities in the prefrontal cortex, resulting in difficulties in sequencing problem-solving steps, detecting and self-correcting errors, and inhibiting irrelevant associations from entering working memory. The other form of retrieval deficit—difficulties in fact access—appears to result from damage to or neurodevelopmental abnormalities in the posterior regions of the left hemisphere and some subcortical structures, such as the basal ganglia. However, with AD children and learning-disabled children in general, neurological deficits are typically presumed and often not concretely demonstrated. Neuroimaging studies with older children or adults with AD would add greatly to the understanding of the brain systems that support basic quantitative abilities in general and AD in particular.

REFERENCES

Ackerman, P.T., & Dykman, R.A. (1995). Reading-disabled students with and without comorbid arithmetic disability. *Developmental Neuropsychology, 11*, 351–371.

Ashcraft, M.H. (1982). The development of mental arithmetic: A chronometric approach. *Developmental Review, 2*, 213–236.

Ashcraft, M.H. (1995). Cognitive psychology and simple arithmetic: A review and summary of new directions. *Mathematical Cognition, 1*, 3–34.

Ashcraft, M.H., & Fierman, B.A. (1982). Mental addition in third, fourth, and sixth graders. *Journal of Experimental Child Psychology, 33*, 216–234.

Ashcraft, M.H., Yamashita, T.S., & Aram, D.M. (1992). Mathematics performance in left and right brain-lesioned children. *Brain and Cognition, 19*, 208–252.

Badian, N.A. (1983). Dyscalculia and nonverbal disorders of learning. In H.R. Myklebust (Ed.), *Progress in learning disabilities* (Vol. 5, pp. 235–264). New York: Stratton.

Barrouillet, P., Fayol, M., & Lathulière, E. (1997). Selecting between competitors in multiplication tasks: An explanation of the errors produced by adolescents with learning disabilities. *International Journal of Behavioral Development, 21*, 253–275.

Briars, D., & Siegler, R.S. (1984). A featural analysis of preschoolers' counting knowledge. *Developmental Psychology, 20*, 607–618.

Bull, R., & Johnston, R.S. (1997). Children's arithmetical difficulties: Contributions from processing speed, item identification, and short-term memory. *Journal of Experimental Child Psychology, 65*, 1–24.

Bull, R., Johnston, R.S., & Roy, J.A. (1999). Exploring the roles of the visual-spatial sketch pad and central executive in children's arithmetical skills: Views from cognition and developmental neuropsychology. *Developmental Neuropsychology, 15*, 421–442.

Carpenter, T.P., & Moser, J.M. (1984). The acquisition of addition and subtraction concepts in grades one through three. *Journal for Research in Mathematics Education, 15*, 179–202.

Conway, A.R.A., & Engle, R.W. (1994). Working memory and retrieval: A resource-dependent inhibition model. *Journal of Experimental Psychology: General, 123,* 354–373.

Dehaene, S. (1992). Varieties of numerical abilities. *Cognition, 44*, 1–42.

Dehaene, S., & Cohen, L. (1991). Two mental calculation systems: A case study of severe acalculia with preserved approximation. *Neuropsychologia, 29*, 1045–1074.

Dehaene, S., & Cohen, L. (1995). Towards an anatomical and functional model of number processing. *Mathematical Cognition, 1*, 83–120.

Dehaene, S., & Cohen, L. (1997). Cerebral pathways for calculation: Double dissociation between rote verbal and quantitative knowledge of arithmetic. *Cortex, 33*, 219–250.

Denckla, M.B., & Rudel, R.G. (1976). Rapid 'automatized' naming (R.A.N.): Dyslexia differentiated from other learning disabilities. *Neuropsychologia, 14*, 471–479.

Fuson, K.C. (1982). An analysis of the counting-on solution procedure in addition. In T.P. Carpenter, J.M. Moser, & T.A. Romberg (Eds.), *Addition and subtraction: A cognitive perspective* (pp. 67–81). Hillsdale, NJ: Lawrence Erlbaum Associates Inc.

Fuson, K.C. (1988). *Children's counting and concepts of number.* New York: Springer-Verlag.

Garnett, K., & Fleischner, J.E. (1983). Automatization and basic fact performance of normal and learning disabled children. *Learning Disabilities Quarterly, 6*, 223–230.

Geary, D.C. (1990). A componential analysis of an early learning deficit in mathematics. *Journal of Experimental Child Psychology, 49*, 363–383.

Geary, D.C. (1993). Mathematical disabilities: Cognitive, neuropsychological, and genetic components. *Psychological Bulletin, 114*, 345–362.

Geary, D.C. (1994). *Children's mathematical development: Research and practical applications.* Washington, DC: American Psychological Association.

Geary, D.C. (1995). Reflections of evolution and culture in children's cognition: Implications for mathematical development and instruction. *American Psychologist, 50*, 24–37.

Geary, D.C., Bow-Thomas, C.C., & Yao, Y. (1992). Counting knowledge and skill in cognitive addition: A comparison of normal and mathematically disabled children. *Journal of Experimental Child Psychology, 54*, 372–391.

Geary, D.C., & Brown, S.C. (1991). Cognitive addition: Strategy choice and speed-of-processing differences in gifted, normal, and mathematically disabled children. *Developmental Psychology, 27*, 398–406.

Geary, D.C., Brown, S.C., & Samaranayake, V.A. (1991). Cognitive addition: A short longitudinal study of strategy choice and speed-of-processing differences in normal and mathematically disabled children. *Developmental Psychology, 27*, 787–797.

Geary, D.C., Hamson, C.O., & Hoard, M.K. (2000). Numerical and arithmetical cognition: A longitudinal study of process and concept deficits in children with learning disability. *Journal of Experimental Child Psychology, 77*, 236–263.

Geary, D.C., Hoard, M.K., & Hamson, C.O. (1999). Numerical and arithmetical cognition: Patterns of functions and deficits in children at risk for a mathematical disability. *Journal of Experimental Child Psychology, 74*, 213–239.

Geary, D.C., Widaman, K.F., Little, T.D., & Cormier, P. (1987). Cognitive addition: Comparison of learning disabled and academically normal elementary school children. *Cognitive Development, 2*, 249–269.

Gelman, R., & Gallistel, C.R. (1978). *The child's understanding of number.* Cambridge, MA: Harvard University Press.

Girelli, L., Delazer, M., Semenza, C., & Denes, G. (1996). The representation of arithmetical facts: Evidence from two rehabilitation studies. *Cortex, 32*, 49–66.

Groen, G.J., & Parkman, J.M. (1972). A chronometric analysis of simple addition. *Psychological Review, 79*, 329–343.

Gross-Tsur, V., Manor, O., & Shalev, R.S. (1996). Developmental dyscalculia: Prevalence and demographic features. *Developmental Medicine and Child Neurology, 38*, 25–33.

Hitch, G.J., & McAuley, E. (1991). Working memory in children with specific arithmetical learning disabilities. *British Journal of Psychology, 82*, 375–386.

Hittmair-Delazer, M., Sailer, U., & Benke, T. (1995). Impaired arithmetic facts but intact conceptual knowledge—a single-case study of dyscalculia. *Cortex, 31*, 139–147.

Hoard, M.K., Geary, D.C., & Hamson, C.O. (1999). Numerical and arithmetical cognition: Performance of low- and average-IQ children. *Mathematical Cognition, 5*, 65–91.

Hynd, G.W., & Semrud-Clikeman, M. (1989). Dyslexia and brain morphology. *Psychological Bulletin, 106*, 447–482.

Jordan, N.C., Levine, S.C., & Huttenlocher, J. (1995). Calculation abilities in young children with different patterns of cognitive functioning. *Journal of Learning Disabilities, 28*, 53–64.

Jordan, N.C., & Montani, T.O. (1997). Cognitive arithmetic and problem solving: A comparison of children with specific and general mathematics difficulties. *Journal of Learning Disabilities, 30*, 624–634.

Koontz, K.L., & Berch, D.B. (1996). Identifying simple numerical stimuli: Processing inefficiencies exhibited by arithmetic learning disabled children. *Mathematical Cognition, 2*, 1–23.

Kosc, L. (1974). Developmental dyscalculia. *Journal of Learning Disabilities, 7*, 164–177.

Levin, H.S., Scheller, J., Rickard, T., Grafman, J., Martinkowski, K., Winslow, M., & Mirvis, S. (1996). Dyscalculia and dyslexia after right hemispheric injury in infancy. *Archives of Neurology, 53*, 88–96.

Luria, A.R. (1980). *Higher cortical functions in man* (2nd Edn.). New York: Basic Books.

McCloskey, M. (1992). Cognitive mechanisms in numerical processing: Evidence from acquired dyscalculia. *Cognition, 44*, 107–157.

McCloskey, M., Caramazza, A., & Basili, A. (1985). Cognitive mechanisms in number processing and calculation: Evidence from dyscalculia. *Brain and Cognition, 4*, 171–196.

McCloskey, M., & Macaruso, P. (1995). Representing and using numerical information. *American Psychologist, 50*, 351–363.

McCloskey, M., Sokol, S.M., & Goodman, R.A. (1986). Cognitive processes in verbal-number production: Inferences from the performance of brain-damaged subjects. *Journal of Experimental Psychology: General, 115*, 307–330.

Morris, R.D., Stuebing, K.K., Fletcher, J.M., Shaywitz, S.E., Lyon, G.R., Shankweiler, D.P., Katz, L., Francis, D.J., & Shaywitz, B.A. (1998). Subtypes of reading disability: Variability around a phonological core. *Journal of Educational Psychology, 90*, 347–373.

Olson, R., Wise, B., Conners, F., Rack, J., & Fulker, D. (1989). Specific deficits in component reading and language skills: Genetic and environmental influences. *Journal of Learning Disabilities, 22*, 339–348.

Ostad, S.A. (1997). Developmental differences in addition strategies: A comparison of mathematically disabled and mathematically normal children. *British Journal of Educational Psychology, 67*, 345–357.

Ostad, S.A. (1998). Developmental differences in solving simple arithmetic word problems and simple number-fact problems: A comparison of mathematically normal and mathematically disabled children. *Mathematical Cognition, 4*, 1–19.

Pesenti, M., Seron, X., & Van der Linden, M. (1994). Selective impairment as evidence for mental organisation of arithmetical facts: BB, a case of preserved subtraction? *Cortex, 30*, 661–671.

Räsänen, P., & Ahonen, T. (1995). Arithmetic disabilities with and without reading difficulties: A comparison of arithmetic errors. *Developmental Neuropsychology, 11*, 275–295.

Rourke, B.P. (1993). Arithmetic disabilities, specific and otherwise: A neuropsychological perspective. *Journal of Learning Disabilities, 26*, 214–226.

Rourke, B.P., & Finlayson, M.A.J. (1978). Neuropsychological significance of variations in patterns of academic performance: Verbal and visual-spatial abilities. *Journal of Abnormal Child Psychology, 6*, 121–133.

Russell, R.L., & Ginsburg, H.P. (1984). Cognitive analysis of children's mathematical difficulties. *Cognition and Instruction, 1*, 217–244.

Semenza, C., Miceli, L., & Girelli, L. (1997). A deficit for arithmetical procedures: Lack of knowledge or lack of monitoring? *Cortex, 33*, 483–498.

Seron, X., Deloche, G., Ferrand, I., Cornet, J.-A., Frederix, M., & Hirsbrunner, T. (1991). Dot counting by brain damaged subjects. *Brain and Cognition, 17*, 116–137.

Seron, X., & Fayol, M. (1994). Number transcoding in children: A functional analysis. *British Journal of Developmental Psychology, 12*, 281–300.

Shankweiler, D., Crain, S., Katz, L., Fowler, A.E., Liberman, A.M., Brady, S.A., Thornton, R., Lundquist, E., Dreyer, L., Fletcher, J.M., Stuebing, K.K., Shaywitz, S.E., & Shaywitz, B.A. (1995). Cognitive profiles of reading-disabled children: Comparison of language skills in phonology, morphology, and syntax. *Psychological Science, 6*, 149–156.

Siegler, R.S. (1987). The perils of averaging data over strategies: An example from children's addition. *Journal of Experimental Psychology: General, 116*, 250–264.

Siegler, R.S. (1988). Individual differences in strategy choices: Good students, not-so-good students, and perfectionists. *Child Development, 59*, 833–851.

Siegler, R.S. (1996). *Emerging minds: The process of change in children's thinking.* New York: Oxford University Press.

Siegler, R.S., & Shrager, J. (1984). Strategy choice in addition and subtraction: How do children know what to do? In C. Sophian (Ed.), *Origins of cognitive skills* (pp. 229–293). Hillsdale, NJ: Lawrence Erlbaum Associates Inc.

Svenson, O., & Broquist, S. (1975). Strategies for solving simple addition problems: A comparison of normal and subnormal children. *Scandinavian Journal of Psychology, 16*, 143–151.

Temple, C.M. (1989). Digit dyslexia: A category-specific disorder in developmental dyscalculia. *Cognitive Neuropsychology, 6*, 93–116.

Temple, C.M. (1991). Procedural dyscalculia and number fact dyscalculia: Double dissociation in developmental dyscalculia. *Cognitive Neuropsychology, 8*, 155–176.

Temple, E., & Posner, M.I. (1998). Brain mechanisms of quantity are similar in 5-year-old children and adults. *Proceedings of the National Academy of Sciences USA, 95*, 7836–7841.

Welsh, M.C., & Pennington, B.F. (1988). Assessing frontal lobe functioning in children: Views from developmental psychology. *Developmental Neuropsychology, 4*, 199–230.

Transcoding and calculation in aphasia

Margarete Delazer and Lisa Bartha

University Clinic of Neurology, Innsbruck, Austria

Aphasia may have deteriorating effects on several numerical skills, such as counting, reading numerals aloud, or writing them to dictation, as these abilities rely on intact language. However, aphasia also seems to have specific effects on the calculation system. Group studies, as well as single-case studies, point to the fact that language-impaired patients have particular difficulties in completing multiplication tasks, while other operations are less impaired. From a theoretical point of view, there is still a debate as to whether this association reflects a general psycholinguistic problem, the effect of aphasia on numerical cognition, or a deficit in non-specific resources underlying both number and language domains. In studies on number transcoding multi-route models have been proposed which parallel semantic and asemantic routes in alphabetical processing. Yet, the review of the empirical evidence suggests that these models still lack relevant theoretical specification.

INTRODUCTION

Aphasic patients frequently have difficulties dealing with numbers, i.e., counting, transcoding numerals between different codes, or answering computations in verbal or written format. This is particularly true for tasks requiring verbal input or output processes. In fact, many numerical skills, such as counting, reading numerals aloud, or writing them to dictation unquestionably rely on intact language processing (Seron & Noël, 1992). There is considerable debate, however, as to whether aphasia has a genuine deteriorating effect on central processes of numerical cognition, in particular on the retrieval of basic arithmetic facts.

Before discussing the relation between aphasia and calculation deficits, we briefly summarise the characteristics of the symbolic systems underlying numerical processing and their relations to language in general. Numbers may be expressed in various forms, such as number words (whether in alphabetical form or in phonological form), Arabic numerals, Roman numerals, arrays of dots, or finger patterns. We will consider in turn the properties of the two most common codes, Arabic numerals and verbal number words.

Arabic numerals constitute a semiotic system that differs from alphabetic language in several respects (Grewel, 1952, 1969; Power & Longuet-Higgins, 1978), but also shares some similarities. Each single element of Arabic script has a meaning in itself, for example the symbol *4* denotes the concept expressed by the word "four". In contrast, single elements of alphabetical script, e.g., the letter "A", do not have meaning by themselves. The system of Arabic notation is a strict one, i.e., the symbols for the digits, such as *2*, and for the operations, such as + or ×, allow only one interpretation (Grewel, 1969). In contrast, language in general has multiple referents (this is valid for common

Address correspondence to: Margarete Delazer, University Clinic of Neurology, Innsbruck, Austria.

The authors are grateful to Luisa Girelli for helpful comments on a first version of the manuscript.

names, but not for proper names). Numerical symbols may be combined and manipulated according to exactly defined rules that are specific to the notational system. The Arabic notation has a very restricted lexicon, using only 10 different symbols. The first nine numbers are represented by nine different digits; from ten onwards, the place value system is introduced. Thus, the quantity expressed by the single digits within a complex numeral depends on their position in the sequence—the rightmost digit representing the units. 0 is used to indicate the absence of a quantity, but also to function as a "place filler", as in *301* (3 hundreds, 0 tens, 1 unit). Both the identity of single elements (digits) and the position of the single elements within the number carry meaning. The two dimensions (identity and position of the digit) are elaborated separately in transcoding to other codes as suggested in neuropsychological (e.g., Deloche & Seron, 1982a,b; McCloskey & Caramazza, 1987; McCloskey, Caramazza, & Basili, 1985; Noël & Seron, 1995) and developmental studies (Power & Dal Martello, 1990; Seron, Deloche, & Noël, 1992; Seron & Fayol, 1994).

In the verbal code (graphemic or phonemic) numbers are expressed by single words (e.g., nine) or by strings of words (e.g., seventy-three). Although the number of single lexical elements is higher than in the Arabic notation, it is still very limited and includes units (from one to nine), teens (from ten to nineteen), tens (from twenty to ninety) and multipliers (hundred, thousand...). Moreover, the order of elements is exactly defined and thus contrasts to most other lexical classes (exceptions are other ordered classes, such as days of the week, months of the year, or music notes). Single number words or *lexical primitives* (Seron & Noël, 1992) may be combined to assemble more complex numerals. The ordering of lexical primitives within a complex numeral is defined by the number syntax (Power & Longuet-Higgins, 1978) which specifies the relation between semantic content and lexical realisation. In particular, lexical primitives are represented in sum or product relations. For example, *three thousand* means three *times* thousand and thus represents a product relation, whereas *twenty three* means twenty *plus* three and accordingly constitutes a sum relation. Number syntax specifies the order of single lexical elements and allows us to discriminate legal (e.g., twenty three) from non-legal numbers (e.g., three twenty).

Overall, both notations, Arabic and verbal, are characterised by a restricted, strictly ordered lexicon with high-frequency elements (Dehaene & Mehler, 1992) and by an exactly defined syntax. One may speculate whether these characteristics lead to particular difficulties in aphasic subjects affecting the production and comprehension of numerical stimuli. While the limited number and the high frequency (both Arabic and verbal) may facilitate the retrieval of lexical elements, the strict one-to-one correspondence between semantic content and lexical output certainly inhibits verbal production, allowing no circumlocution and no ambiguity. The strict sequential order of numerical elements in the lexicon may present further difficulties. In fact, it has been reported that other lexical classes meeting similar linguistic criteria as number words (days of the week or months of the year) lead to qualitatively similar errors (Deloche & Seron, 1984).

Difficulties may also arise from syntactic processing in the comprehension and production of complex numerals. Syntactic processing of numerals is not only a multi-step process and thus error prone, but is also strictly defined and allows no simplifications or alterations. Even slight alterations of number syntax or morphology change the meaning of a numeral. For example, *hundred-four* is different from *four-hundred* and *sixty* is different from the phonologically similar *sixteen*. In conclusion, processing numerals, both in Arabic and verbal code, puts high demands on the language system and may be particularly difficult for aphasic patients.

Research on numerical skills in aphasia is not only of theoretical interest, but has eminent practical relevance. Although the topic has gained more interest in the last few years, there are still surprisingly few studies concerned with the particular difficulties of aphasic patients in numerical tasks. Text books on aphasia rarely address specific problems in number processing. In a short overview of ten standard books on language and aphasia we found nothing specific on number processing in five of them (Caplan, 1992; Code, 1989; Goodglass, 1993; Levelt, 1989; Nickels, 1997), and a single paragraph in three of them (Patterson & Shewell, 1987 [in Coltheart, Sartori, & Job, 1987]; Poeck, 1989; Van Hout, 1999 [in Fabbro, 1999]). A whole chapter is devoted to numbers only in Kaplan and Goodglass (1981; in Sarno, 1981) and Leischner (1987). However, these chapters were written more than ten years ago and cannot account for recent developments.

Unfortunately, the lack of theoretical consideration in standard text books is reflected by a lack of attention in clinical assessment and rehabilitation. Difficulties in number processing certainly do not gain the attention that is demanded by their practical importance, leading to severe handicaps in everyday life. In multi-professional teams of specialists very often nobody is responsible (or specifically trained) for the evaluation and rehabilitation of numerical disorders. Accordingly, rehabilitation of number processing is sometimes performed by speech therapists, sometimes by psychologists, sometimes by occupational therapists, and much too often by no one at all.

HISTORICAL OVERVIEW

Since the last decade of the 19th century, several case reports of patients with calculation disorders appeared and a number of studies attempted to investigate the relation between numerical skills and verbal processing (e.g., Bastian, 1898). Indeed, in the early days difficulties in number processing were generally considered as part of aphasic syndromes and were thought to indicate a general cognitive decline associated with aphasia (Marie, 1906). In 1908, Lewandowsky and Stadelman first described a patient with a specific calculation disorder. Importantly, they suggested that calculation may be impaired without a reduced general intelligence and without aphasic problems. Their patient, a 27-year-old clerk who spontaneously suffered a left occipital haematoma, was perfectly able to write and read Arabic numerals (up to six- and seven-digit numerals), but was severely impaired in simple calculation. Interestingly, the patient seemed to recall the multiplication tables better than simple addition and subtraction facts. Thereafter, other cases of dyscalculia were described (Poppelreuther, 1917; Sittig, 1917; Peritz, 1918). Most of the cases confirmed the importance of the left posterior areas for calculation and found associations between acalculia and language deficits, as well as visuo-spatial deficits.

In 1919 Henschen introduced the term *acalculia* and proposed the first systematic classification of acalculia. Based on a large sample of patients affected by calculation disorders, he suggested that disorders in reading, writing, or pronouncing numbers should be differentiated from mental calculation. He also proposed different cortical centres dedicated to different aspects of calculation and number processing. Henschen stressed that acalculia and aphasia may sometimes be associated, but also that acalculia constitutes an independent symptom.

Shortly after Henschen's contribution, Berger (1926) introduced the distinction between primary and secondary acalculia. The latter would frequently occur in patients with language, attentional, or memory deficits. Primary or "pure" acalculia, on the other hand, would not relate to any other cognitive deficit. Although some of the early studies on acalculia also stressed the role of visual and spatial processing in number processing (Lewandowsky & Stadelmann, 1908; Poppelreuther, 1917; Peritz, 1918), spatial processing was more emphasised in later studies published in the 1930s (Singer & Low; 1933; Kleist, 1934; Krapf, 1937). Difficulties in number processing were also seen as a consequence of an underlying disturbance in body schema. Dyscalculia is, besides agraphia, right–left disorientation and finger agnosia, one of the symptoms that define the Gerstmann syndrome arising after left parietal lesions (Gerstmann 1927, 1930, 1940; for critical views see Poeck & Orgass, 1966; Benton, 1987). Gerstmann assumed that finger agnosia is the core deficit of all four symptoms and that all of them, including acalculia, can be attributed to a disorder of body schema.

Overall, it became clear that calculation disturbance cannot be attributed to a deficit in a single underlying function or to a general intellectual disorder. In fact, in 1961, Hécaen, Angelergues, and Houllier published a large group study including 183 patients and suggested a classification that takes account of different underlying deficits. Similarly to Berger (1926), they classified acalculic patients into three groups: (a) Digit alexia and agraphia with or without alexia and agraphia for alphabetic stimuli. In this group arithmetic operations are affected by difficulties in reading and writing. (b) Spatial dyscalculia. Written calculation is affected by the inability to keep the correct spatial order and the appropriate position of numbers. (c) The last group of patients would be affected by "anarithmetia", where the calculation difficulties are not attributable to one of the deficits mentioned in the other two groups. Hecaen et al. acknowledge that acalculia and aphasia may dissociate. They also note, however, that digit alexia and agraphia are likely to co-occur with language disorders.

In a frequently quoted study Benson and Denckla (1969) analysed the calculation performance of two aphasic patients. Their calculation deficits appeared rather severe when verbal or written answers were requested. When confronted with multiple choice tasks, however, both patients were able to select correct solutions. In both cases Benson and Denckla (1969) identified verbal paraphasias as the source of wrong answers in calculation tasks. They emphasised that even subtle aphasic symptoms may affect performance in calculation tasks and that verbal paraphasias may lead to the misinterpretation of patients' calculation deficits. Benson and Denckla (1969) stressed that incorrect answers in calculation tasks alone cannot be accepted as evidence of acalculia, in particular if only one mode of presentation and one of response is tested. Only careful examination of different modalities and different types of tasks, including multiple choice tasks, would allow a well grounded assessment of calculation abilities. Benson and Denckla (1969) noted that many previously reported cases of acalculia showed word-finding difficulties and hypothesised that paraphasias were a major factor in previously described "pure" calculation deficits.

TRANSCODING BETWEEN DIFFERENT NUMBER CODES

Group studies in aphasia

Deloche and Seron investigated the ability of aphasic patients to transcode integer quantities from written number words to Arabic numerals (Deloche & Seron,1982a,b) and vice versa (Seron & Deloche, 1983, 1984). Their results indicated that Broca's and Wernicke's aphasic patients were differentially impaired in a way that paralleled the general linguistic deficits of the two types of aphasia—Broca's presenting difficulties in syntactic processing, Wernicke's presenting difficulties in lexical processing. Errors were analysed according to the class structure of the verbal number lexicon. Broca's errors consisted frequently in so called class errors, where the erroneously produced answer respects the lexical position, but not the lexical class. For example, a teens number (*twelve*; second position in the teens class) may be transcoded into a unit number (*2*; second position in the unit class). On the other hand, Wernicke's patients were more likely to produce errors belonging to the same lexical class. These errors, which are mostly close to the correct number, have been labelled as position-within-class errors. For example, the verbal numeral *five* (fifth position, unit class) is transcoded to *4* (fourth position, unit class). The clear difference between Broca's errors resulting primarily from syntactic difficulties and Wernicke's errors concerning the sequential organisation of the numerals, led Deloche and Seron to the conclusion that difficulties in transcoding may reflect the dissolution of linguistic skills in general. In fact, they suggested that despite the formal autonomy with reference to language, the verbal number system and the psycholinguistic procedures of that system are not disrupted independently of other linguistic skills. The studies of Deloche and Seron (1982a,b, 1984; Seron & Deloche, 1983, 1984) had great impact on later research investigating transcoding between number codes. The classification of transcoding errors into lexical (e.g., the number word *fifty-two* is transformed to the Arabic numeral *54*) or syntactic (e.g., the number word *fifty-two* is transformed to the Arabic numeral *502*) failures has become standard in later studies.

A recent investigation on transcoding in aphasic patients (Delazer, Girelli, Semenza, & Denes, 1999) partially confirms the results of the previous studies. As expected, the overall error rate correlated with the severity of the language deficit, global aphasic patients being the most impaired. Broca's and Wernicke's scored similarly at the quantitative level, amnestic aphasic patients showed only mild difficulties. Interestingly, error analysis revealed qualitative differences between the patient groups, pointing to their specific language problems. Broca's patients scored significantly lower in reading Arabic numerals than in reading number words. Thus Broca's errors in reading Arabic numerals cannot simply be explained by speech output problems, but more likely by specific difficulties in assembling complex number words. This hypothesis is also supported by the high incidence of syntactic errors observed in this group (87.5% of Broca's patients made syntactic errors in transcoding tasks). Wernicke's patients, on the other hand, frequently made lexical errors in transcoding tasks. However, it is important to note that Wernicke's patients produced syntactic and mixed errors as well. Although the results of this study clearly point to associations between linguistic impairments in general and difficulties in transcoding, errors were also observed in the performance of non-aphasic patients. Thus, transcoding problems are not bound to aphasia, but may also reflect specific difficulties in number processing.

Single-case studies on transcoding

The view of McCloskey et al. (1985).   In contrast to Deloche and Seron (1982a,b, 1984; Seron & Deloche, 1983), McCloskey and co-workers (McCloskey, 1992; McCloskey et al., 1985) made no specific claims about aphasia and deficits in transcoding. Their studies were specifically concerned with cognitive mechanisms involved in transcoding and calculation and led to a modular cognitive model of number processing (McCloskey, 1992; McCloskey, Aliminosa, & Sokol, 1991a; McCloskey, Harley, & Sokol, 1991b; McCloskey et al., 1985; see also McCloskey, Sokol, & Goodman, 1986; McCloskey, Sokol, Goodman-Schulman, & Caramazza, 1990; Sokol &

McCloskey, 1991; Sokol, McCloskey, & Cohen, 1989; Sokol, McCloskey, Cohen, & Aliminosa, 1991). In this model all transcoding processes pass through a common semantic representation. In comprehension, all numerical input is transformed into abstract semantic representations via notation-specific modules. In production, abstract semantic representations activate notation specific modules which produce spoken number words, written number words, or Arabic numerals. The comprehension and production mechanisms include syntactic and lexical stages which are assumed to operate independently from each other. In this view, numeral comprehension and production is organised in highly specialised, selectively vulnerable modules. In fact, several case studies by McCloskey and co-workers (e.g., Macaruso, McCloskey, & Aliminosa, 1993) reported empirical evidence supporting the cognitive architecture proposed in the model.

Because the attention of McCloskey and co-workers was mainly focused on numerical processes and not on linguistic processes in general, they reported very briefly about the language skills of their patients. However, as can be seen from their case descriptions, most of the patients with transcoding deficits were affected by aphasia or showed difficulties in writing or reading alphabetic script (see Appendix). For example, patient RH (Macaruso et al., 1993), who showed multiple impairments in number processing, was affected by expressive aphasia producing dysgrammatical short phrases and stereotypes. Patient HY (McCloskey et al., 1986) was also aphasic, his spontaneous speech was fluent with word-finding difficulties, and literal and verbal paraphasias. Interestingly, his reading of alphabetical stimuli was also impaired (moderately for words and severely for sentences). His reading of Arabic numerals was characterised by frequent lexical substitutions which respected the same number class (e.g., 52 —→ *fifty-three*). Like HY, JG (McCloskey et al., 1986; McCloskey et al., 1990) made substitution errors in reading Arabic numerals. However, whereas only 4% of HY's lexical substitutions were class errors, 60% of JG's errors were class errors (20 —→ *two*). As McCloskey et al. (1990) suggest, the retrieval process accessed the wrong number lexical class, but the correct position within the class. JG's spoken language and comprehension was essentially normal, although she evidenced impairments in spelling and in reading aloud words and nonwords. For other patients, unfortunately, no assessment of general language skills is reported. The number reading of two patients was studied in detail in order to assess syntactic processing in comprehension and production. Errors by JEs (McCloskey, 1992; McCloskey et al., 1990) consisted mainly in quantity shifts (8900 —→ *eight thousand ninety*) suggesting a deficit in generating and filling syntactic frames for verbal numerals. Patient JS (McCloskey, 1992) committed syntactic as well as lexical errors in reading Arabic numerals. After a careful evaluation of error patterns, it was suggested that JS's syntactic errors stemmed from a deficit in placement of multiplier word specifications in syntactic frames for complex numerals (McCloskey, 1992). Moreover, it was suggested that JS was impaired in the retrieval of phonological number-word representations from the phonological output lexicon, but not in the retrieval of graphemic number-word representations from the graphemic output lexicon, thus pointing to separate output lexicons.

Overall, this short and not comprehensive overview of McCloskey and colleagues' case studies on transcoding shows that patients with very selective deficits in number processing (often affecting a single stage of processing), may show more general linguistic impairments, such as word-finding difficulties or even aphasia. Case descriptions also suggest frequent associations between deficits in reading alphabetical stimuli and Arabic numerals (e.g., McCloskey et al., 1986).

The preferred entry code hypothesis.   Other studies more specifically investigated the role of verbal processing in transcoding and some of them assumed that internal semantic representations may reflect the structure of verbal word forms. Noël and Seron (1993) suggested a preferred entry code hypothesis which postulates that the access to semantic representations may be accomplished either from the verbal or the Arabic code, according to the individual's idiosyncratic preference. They described a moderately anomic patient with difficulties in reading Arabic numerals, who based intact semantic processing on incorrectly transcoded numerals. For example, *236* was read as *two thousand six* and judged superior to *1258*. In this case it was assumed that the verbal form constituted the preferred code to access semantics.

A second case study by Noël and Seron (1995) again questioned the assumption of abstract semantic representations. Patient LR's errors in writing Arabic numerals were of the syntactic type and frequently consisted in literal transcriptions of the verbal word forms (e.g., *one thousand four hundred* ⟶ *1000400*). The qualitative analysis of LR's error pattern indicated that product relationships (e.g., *four thousand* ⟶ [*4×1000*]) were better mastered than sum relationships (e.g., *one thousand four hundred* ⟶ [*1000 + 400*]). Noël and Seron argued that this specific error pattern could hardly be explained within an abstract base-ten production system as proposed by McCloskey et al. (1985) and instead argued for a production model with semantic representations reflecting the verbal word form (e.g., Power & Dal Martello, 1990).

The conclusions of this study converge with other single-case studies on writing Arabic numerals (Cipolotti, Butterworth, & Warrington, 1994; Delazer & Denes, 1998). A dysgraphic patient, CK, whose alphabetic output was restricted to graphemic jargon, gradually improved in writing of Arabic script over 13 months after her stroke (Delazer & Denes, 1998). Errors were almost exclusively of the syntactic type. The qualitative error pattern changed over time from invented algorithms over literal transcriptions of the verbal word form to mostly correct transcoding. In line with previously reported neuropsychological (Cipolotti et al., 1994; Noël & Seron, 1995) and developmental (Power & Dal Martello, 1990; Seron & Fayol, 1994) evidence, sum relations were more difficult to transcode than product relations within complex numerals. This case study also shows that performance in writing may improve differentially for alphabetic and Arabic code.

Multiple routes in transcoding.   In recent years, several studies on transcoding have tried to draw parallels between the processes involved in alphabetic reading and those in Arabic numeral reading. Thus, multiple routes have been proposed in number transcoding corresponding to the semantic and asemantic routes identified in word reading (Shallice, 1988). However, the proposed dissociation between asemantic and semantic pathways in numeral reading meets with both methodological and theoretical problems, and has not yet been conclusively established (for an extensive discussion see Seron & Noël, 1995). Most importantly, no double dissociation between asemantic and semantic processing has been observed till now. In fact, all case studies reported better performance in tasks relying on semantic elaboration and none showed the reverse dissociation. It is thus possible that semantic tasks are simply "easier" than asemantic tasks. Moreover, the distinction between semantic and asemantic tasks is theoretically questionable with regard to numerals. Each so-called asemantic task, such as reading Arabic numerals, can be transformed into a semantic task by accessing the respective numerosity of the numeral (Seron & Noël, 1995).

Cohen, Dehaene, and Verstichel (1994) reported a deep dyslexic patient who showed a dissociation between preserved reading of meaningful numbers and impaired reading of numbers without specific meaning. They proposed a model where familiar (meaningful) and unfamiliar numerals are processed via different pathways, the first along a lexical, the latter along a non-lexical route. The number *1789* (year of the French revolution) would be processed along the lexical routes by French subjects, but not the number *2781*. Familiar numerals would be recognised in the numerical input lexicon and would point to the semantic knowledge associated with the number, whereas the unfamiliar numerals would be processed along the non-lexical surface route. Cohen et al. (1994) assumed that their patient had a specific deficit in the surface route, but processed familiar numerals along the lexical pathway. Seron and Noël (1995) proposed an alternative explanation for this patient's reading pattern. They suggest that the familiarity effect intervenes at the verbal output mechanisms. Familiar numbers may be preassembled in the verbal output lexicon (as other verbal formula) and may thus be easier to produce than other, unfamiliar numerals.

In a study of Arabic number reading in two alexic patients, Cohen and Dehaene (1995) proposed an additional reading route, which would allow access to the magnitude representation associated to any well-formed numerals. Both patients were better in reading Arabic numerals in a number comparison task than in reading the same numbers in an addition task. Cohen and Dehaene (1995) argued that two different pathways were accessed in the two tasks, one asemantic, active in reading numerals in the addition tasks, and one accessing analogue magnitude representations, active in the comparison task (the claim of asemantic transcoding in the addition task relies on the number processing model of Dehaene & Cohen, 1995, which states that simple arithmetic facts are retrieved without access to semantic elaboration).

A multiple route model for number processing was also proposed by Cipolotti (1995; Cipolotti & Butterworth, 1995) in two single-case studies. Patient SF (Cipolotti, 1995) was able to correctly produce spoken number words in tasks assessing numerical knowledge and cognitive estimations, but made numerous errors in reading aloud Arabic numerals. The model of Cipolotti and Butterworth suggests two independent pathways for the production of verbal numerals—one asemantic for the reading task and one semantic for the tasks activating number meaning. Seron and Noël (1995) mention similar reservations as in the case of Cohen et al. (1994), most importantly, tasks could be facilitated by the activation of preassembled number words. Interestingly, SF had no language impairment and had no difficulties in reading alphabetical script. The second patient, SAM (Cipolotti & Butterworth, 1995) was mildly impaired in reading alphabetical stimuli and more severely impaired in reading numerals aloud as well as in transcoding tasks requiring written output. In contrast, he was able to correctly produce numerals of the same length in written calculation and two-digit numerals in verbal calculation. Like SF, he was also able to answer tasks tapping numerical knowledge correctly in spoken number words. The observed dissociations between tasks led Cipolotti and Butterworth (1995) to propose direct routes for reading Arabic numerals aloud and for writing Arabic numerals on dictation, which circumvent the central semantic system.

Delazer and Girelli (1997) investigated the reading of number words and of Arabic numerals in ZA, an aphasic and dyslexic patient, over three years. This study particularly focused on the effect of different notation and the effect of different tasks on verbal number production. While a significant improvement was observed in the reading of number words, as well as of other alphabetic stimuli, reading of Arabic notation remained without significant changes over three years. Thus, different codes, Arabic and alphabetic, showed a differential improvement over time. In the second part of the study the effect of semantic information on verbal number production was specifically addressed. Importantly, ZA's verbal number production was significantly better in tasks that involved encyclopaedic knowledge of number and the transcoding of quantities than in asemantic reading tasks. Interestingly, ZA also performed significantly better in reading tasks when asked to attribute a specific meaning to the presented numerals before reading aloud. Thus, the study shows a facilitating effect when semantic information is accessed in verbal number production and, moreover, suggests that this effect cannot be attributed simply to a familiarity or frequency effect at the output level.

In summary, the case studies published in the last few years argue for multiple routes in number processing and challenge the single-route assumption proposed in the McCloskey model. However, these different routes cannot be compared directly to semantic and asemantic reading routes in alphabetic processing. Interestingly, associations between lexical errors in reading Arabic numerals and reading difficulties in alphabetical stimuli were found. For example, the patients described by Cohen et al. (1994) and by Delazer and Girelli (1997) showed marked deficits in reading Arabic numerals and were at the same time unable to read non-words in alphabetical script. Possibly these associations result from a common deficit underlying both tasks, and further investigations may shed more light on the relevance of such associations.

Other case reports point to dissociations between the reading of Arabic and alphabetic script. On the one hand, patient SF (Cipolotti, 1995) showed intact reading of alphabetic script, while the reading of numerals was impaired. On the other hand, patients with pure alexia frequently show preserved reading of Arabic stimuli as compared to reading of alphabetic script (Anderson, Damasio, & Damasio, 1990; Dejerine, 1892). However, the error rates typically increase with multi-digit numerals (Cohen & Dehaene, 1995; Dejerine, 1892; McNeil & Warrington, 1994; Miozzo & Caramazza, 1998). As McCloskey et al. (1990) argue, reading aloud single digits only requires the production of the number word corresponding to the stimulus, a task similar to object naming, whereas reading multi-digit numerals requires the processing of a string of digits and the construction of a syntactically complex sequence. In comparing the two notations, Arabic and alphabetic, one should carefully consider the distinct demands they put on cognitive processing. For example, a deficit in syntactic processing would lead to a dissociation between the processing of Arabic and alphabetic stimuli by affecting Arabic reading, but not alphabetic reading.

CALCULATION AND APHASIA

Neuropsychological models of calculation and their predictions for calculation deficits in aphasic patients

Although all neuropsychological models acknowledge that language and numerical skills are closely linked to each other (e.g., in reading aloud or in counting), they contrast sharply on their assumptions about the role of linguistic processing in calculation. While McCloskey et al. (1985; and following works) propose a modular, abstract calculation system basically not influenced by language, Dehaene and Cohen (1995; Dehaene, 1992) claim that verbal processing is not only crucial in transcoding or counting, but also in calculation. For both models, empirical support has been gathered in recent years which will be discussed in the following section.

McCloskey et al. (1985; McCloskey, 1992) assume a central semantic system that is accessed in all calculation processes independently from the input's format. Thus the model predicts that calculation processes (retrieval of arithmetic facts or multi-digit procedures) are independent from the input format, e.g., 3×4 (Arabic script) and *three times four* (spoken or written number words) are processed in the same central system. Modality-specific effects may only arise from the input modules transforming numerals into abstract representations or in the output modules transforming from abstract representations to numerals (Arabic numerals or number words). The assumption of format-independent calculation processes is supported by the case study of patient PS (Sokol et al., 1991; Sokol & McCloskey, 1991), a patient with a deficit in retrieving multiplication facts. When all combinations of presentation and response formats (Arabic numerals, number words, dot arrays) were systematically varied (e.g., presentation dots, response Arabic digits) PS's error rate was found to be unaffected by stimulus or response format. The data support the hypothesis that arithmetic fact retrieval is mediated by internal numerical representations that are independent of the format. However, as Sokol et al. (1991) acknowledge, this evidence does not prove the assumption of abstract representation, i.e., other internal representations accessed from all number formats would also lead to the same effect. In their view, the assumption of abstract representations would be supported by the nature of calculation errors, in particular the frequent operand errors made by PS (e.g., $7 \times 6 = 48$), which reflect numerical relations rather than phonological similarities.

Dehaene and Cohen (1995; Dehaene, 1992) proposed an alternative to McCloskey et al.'s model. In their model, three different codes are involved in number processing: a visual-Arabic number code, an auditory-verbal code, and an analogue-magnitude representation. The visual-Arabic code mediates digital input and output, multi-digit operations, and parity judgements. The analogue-magnitude code represents the quantity associated with a number as local distributions of activation on an oriented number line. The analogue-magnitude representation underlies number comparison, approximate calculation, estimations, and contributes to subitizing.

The auditory-verbal code represents numbers as syntactically organised sequences of words (Dehaene & Cohen, 1995, following McCloskey et al., 1986). The auditory-verbal code mediates verbal input and output, counting and the retrieval of simple arithmetic facts, in particular multiplication tables, and some additions. The model postulates that simple facts (multiplication and addition) are stored as verbal associations which cannot be retrieved unless the problem is converted into a verbal code. Accordingly, problems presented in Arabic numerals (3×4) have to be converted into a verbal format (*three times four*) before the answer can be retrieved. This direct verbal route is accessed in answering overlearned calculations, in particular for multiplication problems. However, Dehaene and Cohen (1997) also propose a second, indirect route for answering calculation problems. In this indirect route operands are accessed as quantities on the oriented number line where simple calculations can be performed. The indirect semantic route is employed when no verbal association is available, typically for subtraction problems.

Thus, calculation models differ considerably in their assumptions concerning the representation format of arithmetic facts. On the one hand, the semantic model postulates that, whatever the input format, calculation is mediated by an abstract semantic representation (McCloskey, 1992). On the other hand, the triple code model emphasises the role of verbal processing in retrieving arithmetic facts (Dehaene, 1992). A third position, finally, proposes that the number format subserving calculation may vary according to individual preferences (Noël & Seron, 1993). According to individual preferences a subject may access verbal or visual representations underlying calculation.

Language in single-case studies on calculation

The Appendix gives an overview of several recent case studies on calculation and the language examinations they report. As some of these studies centre specifically on calculation they report only scarce data on language processing, making an evaluation difficult. However, from a short inspection of the Appendix it becomes clear that calculation deficits and aphasia are often associated, but also that patients with severe deficits in calculation may show intact language functions.

Dissociations between language and calculation.   In 1982 Warrington reported patient DRC, a consultant physician who, after suffering a left posterior intra-cerebral haematoma, was no longer able to add, subtract, or multiply with any semblance of efficiency. The patient himself described his calculation skills as "having lost all automaticity". He also commented that he reached the solution of simple calculation problems by means of laborious counting strategies. Despite these severe problems in retrieving simple arithmetic facts from memory, DRC showed a normal or near-to-normal performance in a number of additional tasks including approximate calculation, estimation of quantities, or definition of arithmetic operations. Warrington thus concluded that it was DRC's knowledge of arithmetic *facts* and not his knowledge of arithmetic operations that was impaired. The dissociation between arithmetical processing in general and accurate arithmetical computations is the main result of this investigation and has been acknowledged in all later proposed neuropsychological models of calculation. In contrast to the impaired numerical skills, DRC's linguistic skills were found to be preserved. Spontaneous speech was intact, but sometimes ponderous. On a graded-difficulty naming test DRC scored in the superior range, as well as in the Nelson reading test. Only in the Token Test did he achieve lower scores, which were, however, within the limits of normal performance.

Other case studies reporting intact language and impaired calculation concern both deficits in answering arithmetic facts, but also deficits in executing calculation procedures. Arithmetic fact deficits with preserved language have been repeatedly reported within the cluster of Gerstmann syndrome typically arising after left parietal lesions. Two recent case studies of patients affected by Gerstmann syndrome (MAR, Dehaene & Cohen, 1997; JG, Delazer & Benke, 1997) point to severe deficits in semantic understanding underlying their difficulties in simple calculation. Deficits in performing calculation procedures have been repeatedly found in patients affected by frontal lobe damage. Two patients (Luchelli & DeRenzi, 1993; Semenza, Miceli, & Girelli, 1997) showed good linguistic skills in the presence of severe difficulties in monitoring and executing the complex sequence of computational steps. These difficulties contrast with another type of deficit in written calculation, where the complex algorithm itself is not accessible (Girelli, Delazer, Semenza, & Denes, 1996).

In contrast to the cases with preserved language and impaired calculation, Rossor, Warrington, and Cipolotti (1995) reported a patient with good calculation skills whose speech was reduced to a few repetitive and jargon utterances. He also had problems in understanding written and spoken language. Nevertheless he answered addition, subtraction, and multiplication problems in written form and also performed complex multi-digit addition and subtraction without difficulty. Thus, intact language skills do not seem to be a prerequisite for preserved calculation.

Associations between aphasia and calculation deficits.   In many other case studies calculation deficits and aphasic problems are found to be associated. These studies also describe deficits in the retrieval of arithmetic facts (e.g., Sokol et al., 1991) and in the execution of calculation procedures (Girelli et al., 1996). Interestingly, language disorders seem to be more frequently associated to deficits in retrieving multiplication (and sometimes addition) than to deficits in answering subtraction. Several single-case studies reported impaired multiplication in aphasic patients (Dagenbach & McCloskey, 1992; Dehaene & Cohen, 1997; but see Pesenti, Seron, & Van Der Linden, 1994; Girelli et al., 1996; Hittmair-Delazer, Semenza, & Denes, 1994; Sokol et al., 1991), whereas preserved multiplication was found in patients with intact linguistic skills (Dehaene & Cohen, 1997; Delazer & Benke, 1997). Indeed, it has been suggested that multiplication and some additions are mediated by verbal associations, whereas subtractions and divisions, which are not taught systematically, would depend on back-up strategies. In this view, patterns of selectively preserved and selectively disrupted operations are thought to reflect problems in specific levels of processing. Accordingly, language problems should result in a severe deficit in multiplication, but not in subtraction. A problem in executing back-up strategies, on the other hand, should lead to problems in subtraction and division, but not in the overlearned multiplication tables (see Dehaene & Cohen, 1995). Alternatively, it has been proposed that operation-specific deficits result from damage to segregated memory representations (Dagenbach & McCloskey, 1992).

Group studies on calculation and aphasia

Group studies on numerical processing in aphasia often support the view that aphasia may affect central processes of calculation and that intact language supports effective calculation. Kashiwagi, Kashiwagi, and Hasegawa (1987) reported eight aphasic patients with selective deficits in multiplication (addition and subtraction of four-digit numbers were intact). In Japan, multiplication is taught by means of mnemonic rhymes called *kuku*, i.e., via an auditory-speaking route. No matter in what modality a multiplication is presented, the answer is accessed via the verbal *kuku* rhyme. Thus, aphasic difficulties specifically affect the retrieval of multiplication facts. In the study by Kashiwagi et al. (1987), aphasic patients were admitted to a special multiplication training programme and profited most from an approach using the visual writing route.

Two studies compared calculation impairments in different aphasic groups. Dahmen, Hartje, Büssing and Sturm (1982) suggested that Broca's and Wernicke's difficulties in calculation result from different factors, linguistic for the former and spatial for the latter. Rosselli and Ardila (1989) also proposed that distinct underlying deficits may be responsible for the transcoding and calculation impairments in different patient groups. Although all groups (including right hemisphere patients) presented some calculation deficits, the most severe deficits were found in retrorolandic left hemisphere patients. In Rosselli and Ardila's view, calculation represents a specially complex cognitive skill requiring the activity of multiple processes. Accordingly calculation may be disrupted as a result of many different underlying deficits. However, the study did not specifically assess different components of the calculation system. Moreover, summary scores derived from different calculation tasks make it difficult to evaluate the results.

Delazer et al. (1999) reported a group study that aimed to evaluate the relation between aphasia on the one hand and number processing and mental and written calculation on the other hand. Overall, the error rate in various tasks correlated with the severity of the language deficit, global aphasic patients being most impaired. All aphasic patients performed worse than controls in answering arithmetic facts. In all patient groups (amnesic aphasia, Broca's aphasia, Wernicke's aphasia, global aphasia) addition was the better preserved operation. Multiplication was found to be the most impaired operation, in particular in Broca's patients who scored significantly lower in multiplication than in subtraction. While all aphasic groups scored lower than controls in simple fact retrieval, only global and Wernicke's patients scored significantly lower in mental multi-digit calculation and written calculation. The qualitative analysis of written calculation suggested that Wernicke's and global patients had difficulties in retrieving the correct calculation algorithm as well as in the monitoring and execution of complex procedures. Overall, the results of this study are in line with previous studies which stress the role of the left hemisphere in calculation (Grafman, Passafiume, Faglioni, & Boller, 1982; Jackson & Warrington, 1986; Rosselli & Ardila, 1989) and highlight some qualitative differences between aphasic groups.

In conclusion, some single-case studies suggest that calculation and language are mediated by independently working cognitive mechanisms. In particular, selective calculation deficits with intact linguistic functions have been repeatedly reported, pointing to a modular organisation of the calculation system. However, the view of verbally supported calculation skills has also gained empirical support. In single-case studies, as well as in group studies, language and calculation problems were frequently found to be associated. More interestingly, it was found that different types of aphasia may affect calculation skills specifically and do not have a general deteriorating effect. This finding leads to the assumption that aphasic deficits specifically affect components of the calculation system and to the hypothesis that intact language may support the normal working of the numerical system.

Paraphasias and simple calculation

Most single-case studies on aphasic patients have tried to assess numerical processing with a minimum of interference between language and calculation, i.e., to study numerical processes without the disturbing effect of verbal comprehension or production problems. Indeed, as clearly pointed out by Benson and Denckla (1969) paraphasic errors may be highly misleading in the assessment of calculation abilities. In order to avoid this pitfall, most studies on aphasic patients since then have used non-verbal presentation and answer modalities, including Arabic numerals, dot arrays, or pointing from a table. So no attention has been paid to the effect of paraphasias on calculation processes. In fact, aphasic errors offer the opportunity to systematically study the relation between verbal production and calculation, and may be revealing about the processes underlying numerical cognition.

In aphasic patients frequently cannot retrieve the correct phonological form in reading, despite their intact comprehension of the written stimulus. Such patients misread visually presented calculation problems, e.g., for 3 × 4 they read *four times five*. The calculation answers of these patients are particularly interesting, as they provide evidence about the pathways they use, verbal or non-verbal. We present three aphasic patients in whom intact comprehension of arabic numerals dissociates from disturbed verbal production (the first two patients have been reported by Girelli & Delazer, 1999).

BP was a 83-year-old right-handed man, who suffered a left-hemisphere vascular lesion. His spontaneous speech was fluent, but rich in neologisms and paraphasias: the AAT diagnosed a Wernicke's aphasia. BP's reading of Arabic numerals was error-free for single digits and teens only, in multi-digit numerals he also produced illegal verbal numerals (92 ⟶ *dueventi* [two twenty]). In reading number words, visual paraphasias (e.g., *un milione* [million] ⟶ *Milano*) and neologisms (e.g., 35 ⟶ *trententien*) were noted. Writing of Arabic numerals was nearly impossible (5% correct), as was the writing of number words (both on dictation and in transcoding tasks). In contrast, comprehension of Arabic numerals was perfect as indicated by the performance in a number comparison task and in a number composition task (both, 100% correct).

A total of 60 simple calculation problems (20 additions, 20 subtractions, and 20 multiplications) were presented in Arabic numerals. The answer was given verbally and then written down by the patient. BP always read the problems aloud before answering but he produced the correct verbal form only half of the time. Yet he wrote the correct answer to the target problem in 95% of cases, whereas the verbal answer was correct in only 50% of the problems. Thus, the retrieval of the written answer was not affected by the incorrect reading. Seemingly, BP's calculation was not based on verbal processing. This hypothesis is also supported by the fact that verbal errors were never determined by the misreading of the problems. For example, BP read 6×8 as *sei per nove* [six times nine], gave the verbal answer *sessantotto* [sixty-eight] and the written answer *48*.

The performance of the second patient, GS, sharply contrasts to the pattern of BP. GS was a 74-year-old right-handed man who suffered a vascular left-temporo-parietal lesion that lead to Wernicke's aphasia (AAT classification). Spontaneous speech was poor and characterised by perseverations and anomic difficulties, as well as semantic and phonemic paraphasias. GS was error free in the reading of single Arabic digits, but longer stimuli yielded several errors. His reading of number words was characterised by neologisms (e.g., *due* ⟶ *novi*). Writing of Arabic numerals, both on dictation and in transcoding from written verbal to Arabic format, was compromised by lexical difficulties. As in BP, GS's comprehension of Arabic numerals was well preserved, as shown by his performance in a number comparison task and in a number composition task (100% and 83% correct, respectively). Arithmetical procedures were correctly executed. Within simple arithmetic, retrieval of multiplication facts was particularly poor and affected by GS's language problems.

All multiplications from 2×2 to 9×9 were presented four times in Arabic numerals and were answered verbally. GS spontaneously read the stimuli aloud before answering but in 16% of the cases he produced a different problem. In all these cases he retrieved the correct answer to the verbally produced fact; for example, he read "6×9" as *tre per otto* [three times eight] and answered *ventiquattro* [twenty-four]. This type of error was the most frequent (46%), followed by operand (39%), non-table (11%), and table error (4%). Sometimes in reading the problem, GS reversed the order of the operands (e.g., he read 6×9 as *nove per sei* [nine times six]) commenting that some facts sound easier than others.

The description of the two patients shows that there are clear individual differences in the preferred format used to retrieve arithmetic facts. Yet this preference may not always be consistent within a single subject and patients may indeed rely on more than one route in retrieving arithmetic facts. FS was a 64-year-old right-handed man, who suffered a left-hemisphere parieto-temporal abscess following perforation through crutch-field-extension. His spontaneous speech was fluent but revealed frequent word-finding difficulties, phonemic paraphasias, and conduite d'approche. Formal testing with the AAT indicated conduction aphasia, which improved considerably over the following months. Reading and writing of Arabic two digit-numbers was correct in 93% of cases (both 84/90).

FS's deficit in retrieving arithmetical facts mainly concerned multiplication tables. In a first assessment he answered 92% correct in addition (132/144 correct) and 95% in subtraction (174/184), but only 63% correct in multiplication (91/144).

In a series of production tasks in which the modality of presentation and the modality of answer were systematically varied, FS's performance differed only marginally (Table 1) being slightly better with visual presentation and verbal plus written answer. Occasionally FS misread the problems due to his verbal output difficulties. Interestingly, he was equally likely to rely on or to disregard the misread problem in retrieving the answer. For example, he read 2×4 as *zwei mal acht* [two times eight] and answered *sechzehn* [sixteen] verbally and in Arabic digits. In the same testing session, presented with 3×8 he read *drei mal fünf* [three times five] and answered *vierundzwanzig* [twenty four] verbally and in written form. These two error types were equally frequent ($n = 9$) in 100 multiplication problems included in this analysis. Verbal and written answer were not always consistent, although most of the time the written answer followed the verbal output. However, in some cases verbal and written answers dissociated, frequently neither of them being correct. For example, FS read 7×8 correctly, gave the verbal answer *vierundfünfzig* [fifty-four] and wrote 42. Overall, correctly retrieved answers were equally often based on the phonological and the visual problem form.

Summing up, the three case descriptions show that there are considerable individual differences. BP always relied on the visual input despite his verbal paraphasias. SG based his answers on the incorrect phonological forms. FS showed no particular preference and based his answers equally often on the verbal and the visual form, suggesting variability in the processing routes mediating fact retrieval within a single subject. Overall, these results are relevant to the discussion on processing formats in calculation. Whereas answers based on phonological forms would argue for the model proposed by Dehaene (1992), the model of McCloskey et al. (1985) easily explains answers disregarding paraphasic misreading. Taken together, the case descriptions are in favour of a calculation model that contemplates individual preferences in the specific format mediating fact retrieval (Noël & Seron, 1993, 1995).

CONCLUSION

Although several studies have found impaired transcoding and/or calculation in aphasic patients, only some of them specifically discuss the association between linguistic and numerical deficits. From a theoretical point of view, there is still debate as to whether this

TABLE 1
FS's performance in different multiplication tasks

Input	Output	Verbal answer % correct (n = 64)	Written answer % correct (n = 64)
Visual & reading aloud	Verbal & written	67%	67%
Visual	Verbal & written	75%	76%
Visual	Written	–	56%
Verbal	Verbal & written	61%	61%
Writing to dictation	Written	–	66%

association reflects a general psycholinguistic problem, the deteriorating effect of aphasia on numerical cognition, or a deficit in non-specific resources underlying both number and language domains, such as attention or executive control. In many cases it may also be assumed that a large left hemisphere lesion concerns more than one critical area, affecting both language and number processing. However, the different positions do not exclude each other and it is most likely that more than one factor contributes to numerical deficits in individual cases.

Dyslexia for Arabic numerals has been found to show some characteristics often observed in dyslexia for alphabetical stimuli, in particular a dissociation between preserved processing of meaningful stimuli and impaired processing of non-meaningful stimuli. Indeed, these similarities led to the proposal of multi-route models of transcoding which parallel semantic and asemantic routes in alphabetical reading. However, these models certainly need further theoretical specification as well as empirical evidence.

Not only transcoding, but also calculation impairments are frequently associated with aphasia, as shown in several studies. Moreover, aphasia seems to have specific effects on the calculation system. Indeed, group studies, as well as single-case studies, point to the fact that language-impaired patients have particular difficulties in answering multiplication, while other operations, possibly based on non-verbal routines, are less impaired. However, we do not draw conclusions on the verbal basis of calculation in general, as recent case studies report double dissociations between number processing and language. Moreover, individual differences have been mostly neglected in recent research and may present a relevant factor.

Research on calculation in aphasic patients has either specifically focused on numerical processing, assuming a modular cognitive organisation, or studied the relation between language and number impairment at a general level. Yet the effect of paraphasias on simple calculation has been mostly ignored. In three examples we have shown that the analysis of paraphasic errors may be highly revealing about the processing routes in calculation. While one patient ignored paraphasic reading and relied on intact semantic comprehension, another based his answers on verbal calculation routines. A third patient, finally, showed an inconsistent pattern without clear preferences for verbal or non-verbal routines.

Overall, the reported findings lead to straightforward practical implications. First, numerical disorders should be as carefully assessed as language disorders. Second, how language disorder and numerical disorder interact should be evaluated by a detailed analysis of calculation errors. The result of this assessment is the basis on which rehabilitation approaches may be grounded. Of course, the planning of rehabilitation should take into account individual differences—whereas one patient may be encouraged to base answers on non-verbal calculation routines, another may profit from the activation of stored verbal associations.

REFERENCES

Anderson S.W., Damasio, A.R., & Damasio, H. (1990). Troubled letters but not numbers: Domain specific cognitive impairments following focal damage in frontal cortex. *Brain, 113*, 749–766.

Bachy-Langedock, N. (1988). *ExaDé: Batterie d'Examen des Troubles en Dénomination*. Bruxelles: Editest.

Baddeley, A. (1976). *The psychology of memory*. New York: Basic Books.

Badecker, W., & Caramazza, A. (1986). *The John Hopkins Morphology Battery*. Baltimore, MA: The John Hopkins University.

Bastian, H.C. (1898). *A treatise on aphasia and other speech deficits*. London: Lewis.

Baxter-Versi, D.M. (1987). *Acquired spelling disorders*. Unpublished doctoral dissertation, London University.

Benson, D.F., & Denckla, M.B. (1969). Verbal paraphasia as a source of calculation disturbance. *Archives of Neurology, 21,* 96–102.

Benton, A.L. (1987). Mathematical disability and the Gerstmann Syndrome. In G. Deloche & X. Seron (Eds.), *Mathematical disabilities: A cognitive neuropsychological perspective.* Hillsdale NJ: Lawrence Erlbaum Associates Inc.

Berger, H. (1926). Über Rechenstörungen bei Herderkrankungen des Großhirns. *Archiv für Psychiatrie und Nervenkrankheiten, 78,* 238–263.

Bishop, D.V.M., & Byng, S. (1984). Assessing semantic comprehension: Methodological considerations, and a new clinical test. *Cognitive Neuropsychology, 1,* 233–244.

Caplan, D. (1992). *Language: Structure, processing, and disorders.* Cambridge, MA: MIT Press.

Cipolotti, L. (1995). Multiple routes for reading words, why not numbers? Evidence from a case of arabic numeral dyslexia. *Cognitive Neuropsychology, 12,* 313–342.

Cipolotti, L., & Butterworth, B. (1995). Toward a multiroute model of number processing: Impaired number transcoding with preserved calculation skills. *Journal of Experimental Psychology, 124,* 375–390.

Cipolotti, L., Butterworth, B., & Denes, G. (1991). A specific deficit for numbers in a case of dense acalculia. *Brain, 114,* 2619–2637.

Cipolotti, L., Butterworth, B., & Warrington, E.K. (1994). From "one thousand nine hundred and forty-five" to 1000,945. *Neuropsychologia, 32,* 503–509.

Code, C. (Ed.) (1989). *The characteristics of aphasia.* London: Taylor & Francis.

Cohen, L. & Dehaene, S. (1991). Neglect dyslexia for numbers? A case report. *Cognitive Neuropsychology, 8,* 39–58.

Cohen, L., & Dehaene, S. (1995). Number processing in pure alexia: The effect of hemispheric asymmetries and task demands. *Neurocase, 1,* 121–137.

Cohen, L., & Dehaene, S. (1996). Cerebral networks for number processing: Evidence from a case of posterior callosal lesion. *Neurocase, 2,* 155–174.

Cohen, L., Dehaene, S., & Verstichel, P. (1994). Number words and number non-words. A case of deep dyslexia extending to arabic numerals. *Brain, 117,* 267–279.

Coltheart, M., Sartori, G., & Job, R. (Eds.) (1987). *The cognitive neuropsychology of language.* Hove, UK: Lawrence Erlbaum Associates Ltd.

Dagenbach, D., & McCloskey, M. (1992). The organization of arithmetic facts in memory: Evidence from a brain-damaged patient. *Brain and Cognition, 20,* 345–366.

Dahmen, W., Hartje, W., Büssing, A., & Sturm, W. (1982). Disorders of calculation in aphasic patients: Spatial and verbal components. *Neuropsychologia, 20,* 145–153.

De Renzi, E., & Faglioni, P. (1978). Normative data and screening power of a shortened version of the Token Test. *Cortex, 14,* 41–52.

Dehaene, S. (1992). Varieties of numerical abilities. *Cognition, 44,* 1–42.

Dehaene, S., & Cohen, L. (1991). Two mental calculation systems: A case study of severe acalculia with preserved approximation. *Neuropsychologia, 29,* 1045–1074.

Dehaene, S., & Cohen, L. (1995). Towards an anatomical and functional model of number processing. *Mathematical Cognition, 1,* 83–120.

Dehaene, S., & Cohen, L. (1997). Cerebral pathways for calculation: Double dissociation between rote verbal and quantitative knowledge of arithmetic. *Cortex, 33,* 219–250.

Dehaene, S., & Mehler, J. (1992). Cross-linguistic regularities in the frequency of number words. *Cognition, 43,* 1–29.

Dejerine, J. (1892). Contribution à l'étude anatomoclinique et clinique des différentes variétés de cecité verbale. *Mémoires de la Société de Biologie, 4,* 61–90.

Delazer, M., & Benke, T. (1997). Arithmetic facts without meaning. *Cortex, 33,* 697–710.

Delazer, M., & Denes, G. (1998). Writing Arabic numerals in an agraphic patient. *Brain and Language, 64,* 257–266.

Delazer, M., & Girelli, L. (1997). When 'Alfa Romeo' facilitates 164: Semantic effects in verbal number production. *Neurocase, 3,* 461–475.

Delazer, M., Girelli, L., Semenza, C., & Denes, G. (1999). Numerical skills and aphasia. *Journal of the International Neuropsychological Society, 5,* 213–221.

Deloche, G., & Seron, X. (1982a). From one to 1: An analysis of a transcoding process by means of neuropsychological data. *Cognition, 12,* 119–149.

Deloche, G., & Seron, X. (1982b). From three to 3: A differential analysis of skills in transcoding quantities between patients with Broca's and Wernicke's aphasia. *Brain, 105,* 719–733.

Deloche, G., & Seron, X. (1984). Semantic errors reconsidered in the procedural light of stack concepts. *Brain and Language, 21,* 59–71.

Dunn, J.M., & Dunn, L.M. (1981). *The Peabody Picture Vocabulary Test – Revised*. Circle Pines, MN: American Guidance Service.

Fabbro, F. (Ed.) (1999). *Concise encyclopedia of language pathology*. Oxford: Elsevier.

Gerstmann, J. (1927). Fingeragnosie und isolierte Agraphie: Ein neues Syndrom. *Zeitschrift der gesamten Neurologie und Psychiatrie, 108*, 152–177.

Gerstmann, J. (1930). Zur Symptomatologie der Hirnläsionen im Übergangsgebiet der unteren Parietal- und mittleren Occipitalwindung (das Syndrom Fingeragnosie Rechts-Links-Störung, Agraphie, Akalkulie) *Nervenarzt, 3*, 691–695.

Gerstmann, J. (1940). Syndrome of finger agnosia, disorientation for right and left, agraphia and acalculia. *Archives of Neurology and Psychiatry, 44*, 398–408.

Girelli, L., & Delazer, M. (1996). Subtraction bugs in an acalculic patient. *Cortex, 32*, 547–555.

Girelli, L., & Delazer, M. (1999). Differential effects of verbal paraphasias on calculation. *Brain and Language, 69*, 361–364.

Girelli, L., Delazer, M., Semenza, C., & Denes, G. (1996). The representation of arithmetical facts: Evidence from two rehabilitation studies. *Cortex, 32*, 49–66.

Girelli, L., Delazer, M., Semenza, C., & Denes, G. (1997). Calculation and number processing in aphasic patients. *Brain and Language, 60*, 180–182.

Girelli, L., Luzzatti, C., Annoni, G., Vecchi, T., & Cohen, H. (1998). *Progressive decline of numerical skills in Alzheimer-type dementia: A case study*. Poster presented at TENNET IX, the Ninth Annual Conference on Theoretical and Experimental Neuropsychology, Montreal, June 10–12.

Goodglass, H. (1993). *Understanding aphasia*. San Diego: Academic Press.

Goodglass, H., & Kaplan, E. (1972). *The assessment of aphasia and related disorders*. Philadelphia: Lea & Febiger.

Goodglass, H., & Kaplan, E. (1983). *The Boston Naming Test*. Philadelphia: Lea & Febiger.

Goodglass, H., Kaplan, E., & Weintraub, S. (1983). *The Revised Boston Naming Test*. Philadelphia: Lea & Febiger.

Goodman, R., & Caramazza, A. (1986). *The Johns Hopkins Dyslexia Battery and Dysgraphia Battery*. Baltimore, MA: The Johns Hopkins University.

Grafman, J., Passafiume, D., Faglioni, P., & Boller, F. (1982). Calculation disturbances in adults with focal hemispheric damage. *Cortex, 18*, 37–49.

Grewel, F. (1952). Acalculia. *Brain, 75*, 397–407.

Grewel, F. (1969). The acalculias. In P.J. Vinken & G.W. Bruyn (Eds.), *Handbook of clinical neurology* (pp. 181–196) Amsterdam: North Holland.

Hécaen, H., Angelergues, R., & Houllier, S. (1961). Les variétés cliniques de acalculies au cours de lésions rétrorolandiques: Approche statistique du problème. *Revue Neurologique, 105*, 85–103.

Henschen, S.E. (1919). Über Sprach-, Musik- und Rechenmechanismen und ihre Lokalisation im Großhirn. *Zeitschrift für die gesamte Neurologie und Psychiatrie, 52*, 273–298.

Hittmair-Delazer, M., Sailer, U., & Benke, T. (1995). Impaired arithmetic facts but intact conceptual knowledge—a single case study of dyscalculia. *Cortex, 31*, 139–147.

Hittmair-Delazer, M., Semenza, C., & Denes, F. (1994). Concepts and facts in calculation. *Brain, 117*, 715–728.

Huber, W., Poeck, K., Weniger, D., & Willmes, K. (1983). *Aachener Aphasie Test*. Göttingen: Verlag für Psychologie, Hogrefe.

Jackson, M., & Warrington, E.K. (1986). Arithmetic skills in patients with unilateral cerebral lesions. *Cortex, 22*, 611–620.

Kaplan, E., & Goodglass, H. (1981). Aphasia-related disorders. In M.T. Sarno (Ed.), *Acquired aphasia* (pp. 303–325). New York Academic Press.

Kashiwagi, A., Kashiwagi, T., & Hasegawa, T. (1987). Improvement of deficits in mnemonic rhyme for multiplication in Japanese aphasics. *Neuropsychologia, 25*, 443–447.

Kleist, K. (1934). *Gehirnpathologie*. Leipzig: Barth.

Krapf, E. (1937). Über Akalkulie. *Schweizerisches Archiv für Neurologie und Psychiatrie, 39*, 330–334.

Leischner, A. (1987). *Aphasien und Sprachentwicklungsstörungen*. Stuttgart: Thieme.

Levelt, W.J.M. (1989). *Speaking. From intention to articulation*. Cambridge, MA: MIT Press.

Lewandowsky, M., & Stadelmann, E. (1908). Über einen bemerkenswerten Fall von Hirnblutung und ber Rechenstörungen bei Herderkrankung des Gehirns. *Journal für Psychologie und Neurologie, 11*, 249–265.

Lucchelli, F., & De Renzi, E. (1993). Primary dyscalculia after a medial frontal lesion of the left hemisphere. *Journal of Neurology, Neurosurgery, and Psychiatry, 56*, 304–307.

Luzzatti, C., Willmes, K., & De Bleser, R. (1991). *Aachener Aphasie Test: Versione Italiana.* Göttingen: Hogrefe.

Macaruso, P., McCloskey, M., & Aliminosa, D. (1993). The functional architecture of the cognitive numerical-processing system: Evidence from a patient with multiple impairments. *Cognitive Neuropsychology, 10,* 341–376.

Marie, P. (1906). *Travaux et Mémoires, Tome 1.* Paris: Masson.

Mazaux, J.M., & Orgogozo, J.M. (1982). *Echelle d'evaluation de l'aphasie: Adaption française du Boston Diagnostic Aphasia Examination.* Issy-les-Moulineaux, France: Editions Scientifiques et Psychologiques.

McCloskey, M. (1992). Cognitive mechanisms in numerical processing: Evidence from acquired dyscalculia. *Cognition, 44,* 107–157.

McCloskey, M., Aliminosa, D., & Sokol, S.M. (1991). Facts, rules, and procedures in normal calculation: Evidence from multiple single-patient studies of impaired arithmetic fact retrieval. *Brain and Cognition, 17,* 154–203.

McCloskey, M., & Caramazza, A. (1987). Cognitive mechanisms in normal and impaired number processing. In G. Deloche & X. Seron (Eds.), *Mathematical disabilities: A cognitive neuropsychological perspective* (pp. 201–219). Hillsdale, NJ: Lawrence Erlbaum Associates Inc.

McCloskey, M., Caramazza, A., & Basil, A. (1985). Cognitive mechanisms in number processing and calculation: Evidence from dyscalculia. *Brain and Cognition, 4,* 171–196.

McCloskey, M., Harley, W., & Sokol, S.M. (1991). Models of arithmetic fact retrieval: An evaluation in light of findings from normal and brain-damaged subjects. *Journal of Experimental Psychology: Learning, Memory, and Cognition, 17,* 377–397.

McCloskey, M., Sokol, S.M. and Goodman, R.A. (1986). Cognitive processes in verbal-number production: Inferences from the performance of brain-damaged subjects. *Journal of Experimental Psychology, 114,* 307–330.

McCloskey, M., Sokol, S.M., Goodman-Schulman, R.A., & Caramazza, A. (1990). Cognitive representations and processes in number production: Evidence from cases of acquired dyscalculia. In A. Caramazza (Ed.), *Advances in cognitive neuropsychology and neurolinguistics* (pp. 1–32). Hillsdale NJ: Lawrence Erlbaum Associates Inc.

McKenna, P., & Warrington, E.K. (1980). Testing for nominal dysphasia. *Journal of Neurology, Neurosurgery, and Psychiatry, 43,* 781–788.

McNeil, J.E., & Warrington, E.K. (1994). A dissociation between addition and subtraction with written calculation. *Neuropsychologia, 32,* 714–728.

Miceli, G., Burani, C., & Laudanna, A. (1994). *Batteria per l'analisi dei deficit afasici.* Servicio di Neuropsicologia: Università Cattolica di Roma.

Miozzo, M., & Caramazza, A. (1998). Varieties of pure alexia: The case of failure to access graphemic representations. *Cognitive Neuropsychology, 15,* 203–238.

Nelson, H.E. (1982). *National Adult Reading Test.* Windsor, UK: NFER-Nelson.

Nelson, H.E., & O'Connell, A. (1978). Dementia: The estimation of premorbid intelligence levels using the New Adult Reading Test. *Cortex, 14,* 234–244.

Nickels, L. (1997). *Spoken word production and its breakdown in aphasia.* Hove, UK: Psychology Press.

Noël, M.-P., & Seron, X. (1993). Arabic number reading deficit: A single case study or when 236 is read (2306) and judged superior to 1258. *Cognitive Neuropsychology, 10,* 317–339.

Noël, M.-P., & Seron, X. (1995). Lexicalization errors in writing arabic numerals. A single-case study. *Brain and Cognition, 29,* 151–179.

Oldfield, R.C., & Wingfield, A. (1965). Response latencies in naming objects. *Quarterly Journal of Experimental Psychology, 16,* 273–281.

Patterson, K., & Shewell, C. (1987). Speak and spell: Dissociations and word-class effects. In M. Coltheart, G. Sartori, & R. Job (Eds.), *The cognitive neuropsychology of language* (pp. 273–294). Hove, UK: Lawrence Erlbaum Associates Ltd.

Peritz, G. (1918). Zur Pathopsychologie des Rechnens. *Deutsche Zeitschrift für Nervenheilkunde, 61,* 234–240.

Pesenti, M., Seron, X., & Van der Linden, M. (1994). Selective impairment as evidence for mental organisation of arithmetical facts: BB, a case of preserved subtraction? *Cortex, 30,* 661–671.

Poeck, W. (1989). *Klinische Neuropsychologie.* Stuttgart: Georg Thieme Verlag.

Poeck, K., & Orgass, B. (1966). Gerstmann's syndrome and aphasia. *Cortex, 2,* 421–437.

Poppelreuther, W. (1917). *Die psychischen Schädigungen durch Kopfschuss im Kriege 1914–1916.* Leipzig: Voss.

Power, R.J.D., & Dal Martello, M.F. (1990). The dictation of italian numerals. *Language and Cognition Processes, 5,* 237–254.

Power, R.J.D., & Longuet-Higgins, H.C. (1978). Learning to count: A computational model of language acquisition. *Proceedings of the Royal Society (London), B 200*, 319–417.

Rosselli, M., & Ardila, A. (1989). Calculation deficits in patients with right and left hemispheric damage. *Neuropsychologia, 27*, 607–617.

Rossor, M.N., Warrington, E.K., & Cipolotti, L. (1995) The isolation of calculation skills. *Journal of Neurology, 242*, 78–81.

Sarno, M.T. (Ed.) (1981). *Acquired aphasia*. New York: Academic Press.

Schonell, F.J. (1942). *Backwardness in basic subjects*. Edinburgh: Oliver & Boyd.

Semenza, C., Miceli, L., & Girelli, L. (1997). A deficit for arithmetical procedures: Lack of knowledge or lack of monitoring? *Cortex, 33*, 483–498.

Seron, X., & Deloche, G. (1983). From 4 to four: A supplement to "From three to 3". *Brain, 106*, 735–744.

Seron, X. & Deloche, G. (1984). From 2 to two: Analysis of a transcoding process by means of neuropsychological evidence. *Journal of Psycholinguistic Research, 13*, 215–236.

Seron, X., Deloche, G., & Noël, M.-P. (1992). Number transcribing by children: Writing Arabic numbers under dictation. In J. Bideaud, C. Meljac, & J.P. Fisher (Eds.), *Pathways to number* (pp. 245–264). Hillsdale, NJ: Lawrence Erlbaum Associates Inc.

Seron, X., & Fayol, M. (1994). Number transcoding in children. A functional analysis. *British Journal of Developmental Psychology, 12*, 281–300.

Seron, X. & Noël, M.-P. (1992). Language and numerical disorders: A neuropsychological approach. In J. Alegria, D. Holender, J. Junca de Morais, & M. Radeau (Eds.), *Analytic approach to human cognition* (pp. 291–309). Amsterdam: Elsevier).

Seron, X., & Noël, M.-P. (1995). Transcoding numerals from the Arabic code to the verbal one or vice versa: How many routes? *Mathematical Cognition, 1*, 215–243.

Shallice, T. (1988). *From neuropsychology to mental structure*. Cambridge: Cambridge University Press.

Singer, H.D., & Low, A.A. (1933). Acalculia (Henschen): A clinical study. *Archives of Neurology and Psychiatry, 29*, 476–498.

Sittig, O. (1917). Über Störungen des Ziffernschreibens bei Aphasischen. *Zeitschrift für Pathopsychologie, 3*, 298–306.

Snodgrass, J.G., & Vanderwart, M.A. (1980). A standardized set of 280 pictures: Norms for name agreement, image agreement, familiarity, and visual complexity. *Journal of Experimental Psychology: Human Learning, 6*, 174–215.

Sokol, S.M., & McCloskey, M. (1991). Cognitive mechanism in calculation. In R. Sternberg & P.A. Frensch (Eds.), *Complex problem solving: Principles and mechanisms* (pp. 85–116). Hillsdale NJ: Lawrence Erlbaum Associates Inc.

Sokol, S.M., McCloskey, M., & Cohen, N.J. (1989). Cognitive representations of arithmetic knowledge: Evidence from acquired dyscalculia. In A.F. Bennett & K.M. McConkie (Eds.), *Cognition in individual and social contexts* (pp. 577–591). Amsterdam: Elsevier.

Sokol, S.M., McCloskey, M., Cohen, N.J., & Alimonosa, D. (1991). Cognitive representation and processes in arithmetic: Inferences from the performance of brain-damaged subjects. *Journal of Experimental Psychology, 17*, 355–376.

Thioux, M., Ivanoiu, A., Turconi, E., & Seron, X. (1999). Intrusions of the verbal code during the production of Arabic numerals: A single case study in a patient with probable Alzheimer's disease. *Cognitive Neuropsychology, 16*, 749–773.

Thioux, M., Pillon, A., Samson, D., De Partz, M.-P., Noël, M.-P., & Seron, S. (1998). The isolation of numerals at the semantic level. *Neurocase, 4*, 371–389.

Van Hout, A. (1999). Learning disabilities. In F. Fabbro (Ed.), *Concise encyclopedia of language pathology* (pp. 205–213). Oxford: Elsevier.

Warrington, E. (1982). The fractionation of arithmetical skills: A single case study. *Quarterly Journal of Experimental Psychology, 34*, 31–51.

Weddell, R.A., & Davidoff, J.B. (1991). A dyscalculic patient with selective impaired processing of the numbers 7, 9 and 0. *Brain and Cognition, 17*, 240–271.

APPENDIX 1

Some case studies on number processing findings on language & aphasia

Patient	Calculation	Transcoding	Language	Language examination	Reading alphabetic	Writing alphabetic
Cipolotti, Butterworth and Denes, 1991: A specific deficit for numbers in a case of dense acalculia.						
G.C.	n.r.	NUMBER COMPR: impaired for numbers above 4 / ARABIC>PHON: only for numbers up to 4 / PHON>ARABIC: impaired	no aphasia / SS: fluent, but mildly dysarthric / COMPR: normal / PROD: normal	BDAE (Goodglass & Kaplan, 1972; Italian version)	COMPR: reduced / READ: unable to read single letters or words	spelling impaired / unable to write single letters or words
Cipolotti, 1995: Multiple routes for reading words, why not numbers? Evidence from a case of arabic numeral dyslexia.						
S.F.	SIMPLE: A, S: reduced / TWO-DIGIT: A, S: reduced	NUMBER COMPR: intact / ARABIC>PHON: mainly syntactic errors / ALPHA>PHON: intact / PHON>ARABIC: intact / PHON>ALPHA: intact / PHON>PHON: intact	no aphasia / SS: normal / COMPR: normal / PROD: normal	BDAE (Goodglass & Kaplan, 1972; Italian version), Semantic Anomalies Test (Baddeley, 1976); Modified Token Test (De Renzi & Faglioni, 1978); TN: word fluency; reading; naming	READ: intact	writing to dictation skills intact / unable to copy single letters or words
Cipolotti and Butterworth, 1995: Toward a multiroute model of number processing; Impaired number transcoding with preserved calculation skills.						
S.A.M.	SIMPLE: A, S, M: intact / MULTIDIGIT: A, S: intact / M: subnormal	NUMBER COMPR: intact / ARABIC>PHON: syntactic, lexical errors / ALPHA>PHON: syntactic, lexical errors / PHON>ARABIC: syntactic, lexical errors / ALPHA>ARABIC: syntactic, lexical errors / PHON>PHON: intact	aphasia / SS: nonfluent agrammatic, articulation intact / COMPR: normal / PROD: repetition subnormal	Modified Token Test (De Renzi & Faglioni, 1978); Reading Comprehension Subtest of the Boston Diagnostic Ahouse Examination (BDAE, Goodglass & Kaplan, 1972); TN: word-picture matching; repetition; reading; writing	COMPR: normal / READ: mild deficit	impaired

Patient	Calculation	Transcoding	Language	Language examination	Reading alphabetic	Writing alphabetic
Cipolotti, Butterworth, and Warrington 1994: From "one thousand nine hundred and forty-five" to 1000,945.						
D.M.	SIMPLE: A, S, M: intact MULTIDIGIT: A, S, M: reduced	NUMBER COMPR: intact ARABIC>PHON: intact PHON>ARABIC: initially syntactic errors	no aphasia SS: normal COMPR: normal PROD: normal	Graded Naming Test (McKenna & Warrington, 1980); Nelson Reading Test (Nelson & O'Connell, 1978); Schonell Graded Reading Test (Schonell, 1942); Graded Written Spelling Test (Baxter-Versi, 1987)	READ: mild deficit	grapheme omissions, grapheme substitutions
Cohen and Dehaene, 1991: Neglect dyslexia for numbers? A case report.						
Y.M.	SIMPLE: A, M: fairly preserved TWO-DIGIT: A, M: fairly preserved	NUMBER COMPR: intact ARABIC>PHON: positional bias in production of spatial errors, substitutions, perseverations PHON>ARABIC: intact	anomic aphasia SS: fluent, grammatical, word-finding difficulties, semantic and phonemic paraphasias COMPR: good except complex ideational material PROD: naming impaired, automatic speech, and repetition normal	BDAE (French version: Mazaux & Orgogozo, 1982); Modified Token Test (De Renzi & Faglioni, 1978; French translation)	READ: mild deficit	n.r.
Cohen, Dehaene, and Verstichel, 1994: Number words and number non-words. A case of deep dyslexia extending to arabic numerals.						
n.n.	n.r.	NUMBER COMPR: intact ARABIC>PHON: familiar numerals better than unfamiliar, substitution errors ALPHA>PHON: counting strategy	Mild aphasia SS: fluent, informative, phonological paraphasias, word-finding difficulties COMPR: good except complex ideational material PROD: naming and repetition normal, fluency reduced	BDAE (French version: Mazaux & Orgogozo, 1982)	COMPR: various READ: deep dyslexia	impaired

Patient	Calculation	Transcoding	Language examination	Language	Reading alphabetic	Writing alphabetic
Cohen and Dehaene, 1995: Number processing in pure alexia: The effect of hemispheric asymmetries and task demands.						
G.O.D.	SIMPLE: A: visually presented pairs reduced, orally presented pairs intact	NUMBER COMPR: intact ARABIC>PHON: better for two digits as a pair than as a two-digit numeral PHON>ARABIC: intact	BDAE (French version: Mazaux & Orgogozo, 1982); Naming (selected from the set of Snodgrass & Vanderwart, 1980)	no aphasia SS: normal except word-finding difficulties COMPR: good except complex ideational material PROD: normal	COMPR: reduced READ: pure alexia	normal
S.M.A.	SIMPLE: A: visually presented pairs reduced, orally presented pairs intact	NUMBER COMPR: intact ARABIC>PHON: better for two digits as a pair than as a two-digit numeral PHON>ARABIC: intact	BDAE (French version: Mazaux & Orgogozo, 1982), Naming (selected from the set of Snodgrass & Vanderwart, 1980)	no aphasia SS: normal COMPR: normal PROD: normal	COMPR: reduced READ: pure alexia	normal
Dagenbach and McCloskey, 1992: The organization of arithmetic facts in memory: Evidence from a brain-damaged patient.						
n.n.	SIMPLE: far better for S than for A and M in production tasks MULTI-DIGIT: impaired	Arabic NUMBER COMPR: intact Written and spoken NUMBER COMPR: impaired PHON>ARABIC: intact for 1-digit numerals, impaired for longer numerals	BDAE (Goodglass & Kaplan, 1983)	aphasia SS: non fluent, single words and phrases COMPR: impaired PROD: impaired	READ: impaired	impaired
Dehaene and Cohen, 1991: Two mental calculation systems: A case study of severe acalculia with preserved approximation.						
N.A.U.	SIMPLE: A, S, M: impaired	NUMBER COMPR: only for relative magnitude, parity judgement impaired ARABIC>PHON: difficulties, counting strategy	BDAE (French version: Mazaux & Orgogozo, 1982); TN: reading	aphasia SS: n.r. COMPR: moderate impairment PROD: moderate impairment	READ: deep dyslexia	severly impaired writing

Patient	Calculation	Transcoding	Language	Language examination	Reading alphabetic	Writing alphabetic
Dehaene and Cohen, 1997: Cerebral pathways for calculation: Double dissociation between rote verbal and quantitative knowledge of arithmetic.						
M.A.R.	SIMPLE: A,S, M: impaired, S and D more impaired MULTI-DIGIT: A, S: impaired	NUMBER COMPR: intact ARABIC>PHON: intact PHON>ARABIC: intact	no aphasia SS: normal COMPR: normal PROD: normal	BDAE (French version: Mazaux & Orgogozo, 1982)	READ: normal	writing intact oral spelling reduced spelling to dictation reduced
B.O.O.	SIMPLE CALC: A,S: intact M: impaired MULTI-DIGIT: A, S: impaired	NUMBER COMPR: intact ARABIC>PHON: intact PHON>ARABIC: intact	mild language deficits SS: slowed, hypophonic, reduced verbal fluency, word-finding difficulties COMPR: normal PROD: normal except fluency	BDAE (French version: Mazaux & Orgogozo, 1982)	READ: normal	oral spelling reduced serial writing reduced
Delazer and Benke, 1997: Arithmetic facts without meaning.						
J.G.	SIMPLE: M: preserved A, S: impaired MULTIDIGIT: A, S, M: impaired	NUMBER COMPR: intact ARABIC>PHON: intact ALPHA>PHON: intact PHON>ARABIC: slow but preserved PHON>ALPHA: impaired due to severe agraphia ALPHA>ARABIC: intact ARABIC>ALPHA: impaired due to severe agraphia	no aphasia SS: normal COMPR: normal PROD: normal	Token Test (De Renzi & Faglioni, 1978); Aachener Aphasie Test (Huber, Poeck, Weniger, & Willmes, 1983); TN: reading of words and nonwords	COMPR: normal READ: intact	copying letters and writing letters and words on dictation impaired

Patient	Calculation	Transcoding	Language	Language examination	Reading alphabetic	Writing alphabetic
Delazer and Girelli, 1997: When 'Alfa Romeo' facilitates 164: Semantic effects in verbal number production.						
Z.A.	SIMPLE: M: compromised A, S: intact MULTI-DIGIT: M: compromised A, S: intact	NUMBER COMPR: intact PHON>PHON: intact ARABIC>PHON: reduced for multi-digit numerals ALPHA>PHON: reduced for multi-digit numerals PHON>ARABIC: reduced for multi-digit numerals ALPHA>ARABIC: relatively preserved	nonfluent aphasia SS: frequent anomias and severe articulatory problems COMPR: reduced PROD: reduced	Aachener Aphasie Test (Italian version: Luzzatti et al., 1991)	READ: function words and verbs reduced	n.r. (motoric problems)
Delazer and Denes, 1998: Writing Arabic numerals in an agraphic patient.						
C.K.	SIMPLE: A, S, M: improving over time	NUMBER COMPR: intact ARABIC>PHON: improving over time, intact at the end PHON>ARABIC: syntactic errors, lexical errors only in longer numbers	mild amnesic aphasia SS: good COMPR: mildly reduced PROD: reduced	Aachener Aphasie Test (Italian version: Luzzatti et al., 1991)	READ: intact	oral spelling impaired writing of single letters intact, of words impaired
Girelli and Delazer, 1996: Subtraction bugs in an acalculic patient.						
M.T.	SIMPLE: M: compromised A, S: intact MULTI-DIGIT: S, M: compromised A: intact	NUMBER COMPR: intact PHON>PHON: impaired due to impaired language production ARABIC>PHON: limited to single digits ALPHA>PHON: impaired due to impaired language production PHON>ARABIC: limited to single digits ALPHA>ARABIC: intact	global aphasia SS: nonfluent, limited to single words and stereotypes COMPR: mildly impaired PROD: severly impaired	Aachener Aphasie Test (Italian version: Luzzatti et al., 1991)	COMPR: impaired READ: severely impaired	writing severely impaired

Patient	Calculation	Transcoding	Language	Language examination	Reading alphabetic	Writing alphabetic
Girelli, Luzzati, Annoni, Vecchi, and Cohen, 1998: Progressive decline of numerical skills in Alzheimer-type dementia: A case study.						
E.P.	SIMPLE: A,S, M: deteriorating over time	NUMBER COMPR: intact ARABIC>PHON: deteriorating over time ALPHA>PHON: intact PHON>ARABIC: intact PHON>ALPHA: intact ARABIC>ALPHA: reduced ALPHA>ARABIC: reduced PHON>PHON: intact	no aphasia SS: normal COMPR: normal PROD: normal	Aachener Aphasie Test (Italian version: Luzzatti et al., 1991)	COMPR: normal READ: normal	normal
Hittmair-Delazer, Semenza, and Denes, 1994: Concepts and facts in calculation.						
B.E.	SIMPLE: A, S: good M: impaired	NUMBER COMPR: intact PHON>PHON: articulatory difficulties ARABIC>PHON: impaired for long numbers ALPHA>PHON: impaired for long numbers PHON>ARABIC: impaired for long numbers ALPHA>ARABIC: intact	Broca's aphasia SS: nonfluent COMPR: slight impairment PROD: reduced	Aachener Aphasie Test (Italian version: Luzzatti et al., 1991)	READ: reduced	reduced
Hittmair-Delazer, Sailer, and Benke, 1995: Impaired arithmetic facts but intact conceptual knowledge—a single case study of dyscalculia.						
D.A.	SIMPLE: A,S, M: reduced TWO-DIGIT: reduced	NUMBER COMPR: intact ARABIC>PHON: intact ALPHA>PHON: intact	no aphasia SS: normal COMPR: normal PROD: normal	Naming (Snodgrass & Vanderwart, 1980); TN: comprehension; repetition; reading of words and nonwords	COMPR: normal READ: normal	not tested because of hand weakness and ataxia
Lucchelli and De Renzi, 1993: Primary dyscalculia after a medial frontal lesion of the left hemisphere.						
n.n.	SIMPLE: A, S, M: correct but often delayed MULTI-DIGIT: A, S: reduced	NUMBER COMPR: intact ARABIC>PHON: intact PHON>ARABIC: intact ARAB>ALPHA: intact ALPHA>ARABIC: intact	no aphasia SS: limited COMPR: normal PROD: normal	Boston Naming Test (Goodglass & Kaplan, 1983) TN: standardised aphasia battery; Token Test	READ: normal	normal

Patient	Calculation	Transcoding	Language	Language examination	Reading alphabetic	Writing alphabetic
Macaruso, McCloskey, and Aliminosa, 1993: The functional architecture of the cognitive numerical-processing system: Evidence from a patient with multiple impairments.						
R.H.	n.r.	NUMBER COMPR: reduced; ARABIC>PHON: reduced; PHON>ARABIC: reduced; PHON>ALPHA: impaired; PHON>DOTS: reduced; ARAB>ALPHA: impaired; ALPHA>ARABIC: reduced; ALPHA>PHON: reduced; ALPHA>DOTS: reduced; DOTS>ARABIC: reduced; DOTS>PHON: reduced; DOTS>ALPHA: impaired	expressive aphasia; SS: nonfluent dysgrammatical with short phrases and stereotypes; COMPR: reduced; PROD: naming, repetition reduced	BDAE (Goodglass & Kaplan, 1983); Revised Boston Naming Test (Goodglass, Kaplan, & Weintraub, 1983); Subset of items of the Johns Hopkins Dyslexia Battery (Goodman & Caramazza, 1986); Subset of items of the Johns Hopkins Dysgraphia Battery (Goodman & Caramazza, 1986); Morphology Battery (Badecker & Caramazza, 1986)	COMPR: normal; READ: moderate impairment of lexical reading, severe impairment of non-lexical reading	severe impairment
McCloskey, Sokol, and Goodman, 1986 (also in McCloskey, 1992): Cognitive processes in verbal-number production: Inferences from the performance of brain-damaged subjects.						
H.Y.	SIMPLE: A: reduced, more with verbal than with written response	NUMBER COMPR: intact; ARABIC>PHON: lexical substitutions; ARABIC>ALPHA: less reduced	aphasia; SS: fluent, word-finding difficulties, literal and verbal paraphasias; COMPR: normal; PROD: repetition reduced, naming impaired	BDAE (Goodglass & Kaplan, 1972); Boston Naming Test (Goodglass & Kaplan, 1983); Peabody Picture Vocabulary Test (Dunn & Dunn, 1981)	COMPR: impaired; READ: impaired	impaired
J.G.	n.r.	NUMBER COMPR: intact; ARABIC>PHON: reduced; ARABIC>ALPHA: less reduced	no aphasia; SS: normal; COMPR: normal; PROD: naming reduced	Boston Naming Test (Goodglass & Kaplan, 1983); Peabody Picture Vocabulary Test (Dunn & Dunn, 1981)	COMPR: intact; READ: words intact, sentences reduced	oral and written spelling reduced

Patient	Calculation	Transcoding	Language	Language examination	Reading alphabetic	Writing alphabetic
Noël and Seron, 1993: Arabic number reading deficit: A single case study or when 236 is read (2306) and judged superior to 1258.						
N.R.	SIMPLE: impaired	NUMBER COMPR: reduced for Arabic numbers; PHON>PHON: intact; ALPHA>PHON: reduced; PHON>ALPHA: reduced; ARABIC>PHON: reduced, mostly syntactic errors; ARAB>ALPHA: reduced; PHON>ARABIC: reduced mostly for 3-digit numbers; ALPHA>ARABIC: reduced	SS: fluent, moderate anomia; COMPR: normal; PROD: below normal range	Naming Test (Bachy-Langedock, 1988), moderate anomia; TN: Token Test; auditory comprehension; Language Examination Test, reading of letters, words and nonwords; writing	READ: words normal, nonwords impaired	severe deficit, affected by apraxia
Noël and Seron, 1995: Lexicalization errors in writing arabic numerals. A single case study.						
L.R.	SIMPLE: intact	NUMBER COMPR: intact; ALPHA>PHON: intact; PHON>ALPHA: few lexical errors; ARABIC>PHON: reduced; ARAB>ALPHA: reduced; PHON>ARABIC: syntactic errors; ALPHA>ARABIC: syntactic errors, intrusions	SS: perseverations; COMPR: reduced; PROD: poor fluency, naming reduced	n.r.	READ: normal	few spelling errors
Pesenti, Seron, and Van der Linden, 1994: Selective impairment as evidence for mental organisation of arithmetical facts: BB, a case of preserved subtraction?						
B.B.	SIMPLE: A, M: reduced S: relatively preserved	NUMBER COMPR: intact; PHON>PHON: intact; PHON>ARABIC: intact; PHON>ALPHA: intact; ARABIC>PHON: reduced, mainly due to reduced writing; ARAB>ALPHA: reduced mainly due to reduced writing; ALPHA>PHON: intact; ALPHA>ARABIC: reduced	SS: very poor; COMPR: reduced; PROD: reduced	TN: oral and written comprehension; repetition; reading of words, nonwords and sentences; giving definitions and opposites of words; construction of sentences; semantic categorization; spelling; sentence–picture matching; naming; production of automatized verbal sequences, writing	COMPR: intact; READ: normal	altered writing, distorted grapheme production, dysorthography

Patient	Calculation	Transcoding	Language	Language examination	Reading alphabetic	Writing alphabetic
Semenza, Miceli, and Girelli, 1997: A deficit for arithmetical procedures: Lack of knowledge or lack of monitoring?						
M.M.	SIMPLE: A, S, M: intact MULTI-DIGIT: A, S, M: mental calculation intact, arithmetical procedures in written calculation reduced	NUMBER COMPR: intact PHON>ARABIC: intact PHON>ALPHA: intact ARABIC>PHON: intact ALPHA>PHON: intact	no aphasia SS: normal COMPR: intact PROD: intact	Aphasia Battery (Miceli, Burani, & Laudanna, 1994)	COMPR: normal READ: normal	normal
Sokol, McCloskey, Cohen, and Aliminosa, 1991: Cognitive representation and processes in arithmetic: Inferences from the performance of brain-damaged subjects.						
P.S.	SIMPLE: M: reduced, especially problems with 0s MULTI-DIGIT: M: impaired	NUMBER COMPR: intact	SS: severe verbal dysfluency COMPR: n.r. PROD: n.r.	n.r.	n.r.	n.r.
G.E.	SIMPLE: A, M: reduced MULTI-DIGIT: M: impaired	NUMBER COMPR: intact	SS: n.r. COMPR: n.r. PROD: mild naming deficits	n.r.	n.r.	mild deficits in spelling

Patient	Calculation	Transcoding	Language	Language examination	Reading alphabetic	Writing alphabetic

Thioux, Pillon, Samson, De Partz, Noël, and Seron, 1998: The isolation of numerals at the semantic level.

Patient	Calculation	Transcoding	Language	Language examination	Reading alphabetic	Writing alphabetic
N.M.	SIMPLE: A, S: intact M: reduced	NUMBER COMPR: intact PHON>ARABIC: reduced ALPHA>ARABIC: reduced ARABIC>PHON: relatively preserved	severe anomic aphasia SS: fluent, without paraphasias, but non-informative COMPR: reduced PROD: anomia, repetition normal	Picture Naming (Bachy-Langedock, 1988); LUVS (Bishop & Byng 1984, French version); TN: automatic series; lexical decision; picture classification; word–picture matching; word–picture verification; picture naming; naming from definition; written naming; recognition and production of synonyms; verbal fluency; verbal associations	READ: normal	reduced

Thioux, Ivanoiu, Turconi, and Seron, 1999: Intrusions of the verbal code during the production of Arabic numerals: A single case study in a patient with probable Alzheimer's disease.

Patient	Calculation	Transcoding	Language	Language examination	Reading alphabetic	Writing alphabetic
Y.C.	SIMPLE: A, S, M: reduced	NUMBER COMPR: intact ARABIC>PHON: relatively preserved PHON>ARABIC: shift errors ALPHA>ARABIC: shift errors PHON>ALPHA: reduced but only few shift errors ARABIC>ALPHA: reduced but only few shift errors	no aphasia SS: normal COMPR: normal PROD: repetition normal, naming relatively preserved	TN: repetition of letters, syllables, pseudowords, words and sentences; picture naming; auditory comprehension of words and sentences; reading of letters, syllables, pseudowords, words and sentences; writing of words and pseudowords	READ: normal	impaired (orthographic regularisation)

Warrington, 1982: The fractionation of arithmetical skills: A single case study.

Patient	Calculation	Transcoding	Language	Language examination	Reading alphabetic	Writing alphabetic
D.R.C.	SIMPLE: A, S, M: reduced TWO-DIGIT: A, S: reduced	NUMBER COMPR: intact ARABIC>PHON: intact PHON>ARABIC: intact	no aphasia SS: normal but ponderous COMPR: subnormal PROD: normal	Naming Test (McKenna & Warrington, 1980); Nelson Reading Test (Nelson & O'Connell, 1978); Token Test	READ: normal	n.r.

Patient	Calculation	Transcoding	Language	Language examination	Reading alphabetic	Writing alphabetic
Weddell and Davidoff, 1991: A dyscalculic patient with selective impaired processing of the numbers 7, 9 and 0.						
J.C.	SIMPLE: A, S, M: reduced for 7, 9 and 0 TWO-DIGIT: A, S, M: reduced	NUMBER COMPR: intact ARABIC>PHON: intact ALPHA>ARABIC: reduced	no aphasia SS: normal COMPR: normal PROD: normal	Naming (Oldfield & Wingfeld, 1965); Short Token Test (De Renzi & Faglioni, 1978); National Adult Reading Test (Nelson, 1982)	READ: normal	n.r.

n.n. = not named, n.r. = not reported, SIMPLE = simple calculation, MULTI-DIGIT = multi-digit calculation, A = addition, S = subtraction, M = multiplication, NUMBER COMPR = number comprehension, TN = tests not published or quoted, SS = spontaneous speech, COMPR = language comprehension, PROD = language production, READ COMPR = reading comprehension, READ = reading.

APHASIOLOGY, 2001, 15 (7), 681–694

Numerical abilities in dementia

Luisa Girelli

Università degli Studi di Milano-Bicocca, Milan, Italy

Margarete Delazer

Universitäts Klinik für Neurologie, Innsbruck, Austria

The purpose of the present paper is to provide a critical review of the neuropsychological evidence elucidating the incidence and nature of numerical difficulties in dementia. Though long neglected, the occurrence of dyscalculia in the early stage of Alzheimer's disease (AD) has caught the attention of many, and both group studies and single-case investigations converge in identifying number processing and numerical difficulties among the early signs of dementia. Yet analysis of the available data suggests that the pattern of decline may vary greatly across individuals: numerical difficulties may be highly selective and limited to single processing mechanisms but also extended to all aspects of numerical abilities.

Overall, data from AD, in agreement with acquired disorders in focal lesioned patients, confirm the dissociations between multiple functional components of the number processing and calculation system.

INTRODUCTION

Calculation and number-processing abilities are not routinely evaluated for diagnosis of Alzheimer's dementia, neither have they been the object of targeted investigations in this clinical population until recently. Yet, in recent years, the social and daily importance of these competencies has been recognised, motivating the remarkable effort devoted to the study of the cognitive mechanisms underlying numerical abilities. This growing interest is well reflected in the increasing number of studies on acquired numerical deficits. The neuropsychological approach to numerical deficits has mainly concerned the study of patients with focal cerebral lesions, although a few systematic single-case studies on demented patients with highly selective deficits in the numerical domain have been reported. These investigations helped to elucidate the modularity of the numerical and calculation system, showing, on the one hand, its independence from other cognitive functions (e.g., language, memory) and, on the other hand, its internal structure, including multiple independent components. In fact, although dementia frequently results in diffuse cerebral disorders, highly selective neuropsychological deficits may also occur, in particular at the early stages of the illness.

Besides this evidence, a number of recent studies have directly addressed the issue of numerical abilities in dementia either by testing groups of patients suffering from Alzheimer's disease (AD) or by evaluating, in single-case follow-up studies, the pattern

---

Address correspondence to: Luisa Girelli, Università degli Studi di Milano-Bicocca, Dipartimento di Psicologia, Edificio U6, Piazza dell' Ateneo Nuovo 1, 20126 Milano, Italia. Email: luisa.girelli@unimib.it

This research was supported by a Wellcome Grant n. 054721.

http://www.tandf.co.uk/journals/pp/02687038.html   DOI:10.1080/02687040143000122

of preserved and impaired numerical skills as the illness progresses. Group studies have mainly emphasised the role of executive function deficits and limited cognitive resources in determining numerical disorders in dementia. Follow-up studies, on the other hand, have allowed the tracing of the orderly dissolution of numerical abilities in dementia, providing insight into their underlying functional organisation.

The purpose of the present paper is to provide a critical review of the studies that, by means of different methodological approaches, have contributed to our understanding of whether and to what extent numerical disorders characterise the cognitive profile of demented patients. First, the pilot studies carried out on large clinical populations will be reviewed. Then, evidence of AD patients' basic numerical abilities, numerical transcoding, and calculation skills will, in turn, be analysed. A separate section will present data on the selective preservation of calculation skills in otherwise cognitively deteriorated AD patients. Finally, in the light of the examined evidence, we will attempt to provide general conclusions identifying established effects and open issues.

PILOT STUDIES

Several studies have explored the occurrence of numerical and calculation deficits in AD patients by administering a single numerical task as part of extensive neuropsychological batteries (e.g., Kennedy et al., 1995; Parlato et al., 1992). Some others favoured a more detailed evaluation of number-processing and calculation abilities, yet the discussion of the results was limited to the frequency of numerical difficulties and correlation values between these latter and other cognitive functions. Although these investigations may not clarify the time-course or the qualitative changes that characterise the dissolution of numerical skills in Alzheimer's type dementia, they provide relevant data on the incidence of these disorders at different stages of the disease.

Among the more frequently quoted investigations on calculation in AD is the study by Parlato et al. (1992). The authors aimed to evaluate whether dyscalculia may be considered an early sign of Alzheimer's disease, testing a population of 28 probable AD patients whose basic number-processing skills were intact (i.e., reading numerals, numerals comprehension and repetition, counting). To assess mental calculation abilities only two tests were administered, the Stamp Test (ST) and the Serial Seven Subtraction Test (SSST). In both tests, AD patients performed lower than controls; however, the two calculation tasks correlated differently with scores from other cognitive domains: the ST was highly correlated with attention and the SSST with receptive and productive language. These findings are relatively unsurprising given the rather different nature of the ST and SSST tests: if the latter simply requires the computation of sequential subtraction, the former, consisting of an arithmetic text problem, is more demanding in terms of planning and attentional resources. Overall, several reasons render the Parlato et al. contribution inconclusive and unsatisfactory. Of major concern, both tests used to evaluate mental calculation present intrinsic limitations, partially admitted by the authors themselves. The ST consists of a single arithmetic text problem which requires, further to verbal comprehension, memory and planning resources, a mental addition or multiplication, and one subtraction: although the administration of a single trial may be used in a screening procedure, it remains less than informative as an experimental task. On the other hand, the SSST requires the execution of serial subtraction, thus evaluating the ability to compute this operation only. Moreover, the authors' suggestion that calculation difficulties may occur earlier than number-processing deficits in AD seems rather unfounded given that intact numerical processing was one of the selection criteria of the study.

A more exhaustive evaluation of numerical and calculation disorders in AD was carried out by Deloche et al. (1995). They administered to 17 mild AD patients a standardised battery comprising a variety of tasks (n = 31) tapping comprehension and production of numerals in different formats as well as calculation ability. To exclude numerical problems secondary to visuo-spatial deficits, a normal score in a visuo-perceptive test was among the selection criteria. Of the 17 patients, 12 showed impaired overall performance, suggesting that numerical deficits frequently occur in an early stage of AD. Unfortunately, despite the variety of abilities evaluated, results are only discussed in general terms. At the group level, calculation performance correlated with both language and MMSE scores, but not with memory. However, analysis of the single cases indicated different patterns of preserved/impaired abilities with regard to calculation, language, and memory. Similarly, dissociations among different components of the numerical processing and calculation systems suggested heterogeneous profiles of numerical skills deterioration.

Recently, the same standardised battery (EC 301-R, Deloche et al,. 1994) together with tests for language, memory, visuo-spatial abilities, and executive-attentional functions, was administered to 64 mild AD and 242 matched controls (Carlomagno et al.. 1999). Although a variety of tasks testing different aspects of numerical competence were used, the analysis was carried out on four cumulative scores for number production, number comprehension, numerical judgement, and calculation/problem solving, respectively. However, this procedure may very likely produce an oversimplified pattern of results, preventing any information from the single task and dissociations between the tasks from emerging. Indeed, AD patients performed lower than controls in all the four identified arithmetical domains, with a similar number of patients scoring below the cut-off value in all areas. Interestingly, the overall battery scores did not correlate with dementia severity, nor with performance in other cognitive domains except executive-attentional functions. This latter was also related to scores in the different arithmetical domains, apart from number comprehension. On the other hand, a principal component analysis indicated a common factor underlying difficulties in all comprehension tasks. The authors identified this factor as a selective deficit in accessing number semantic representations. This latter combined with a general decline in attentional resources would account for the variety of numerical difficulties observed in AD.

However, a subject by subject analysis disclosed dissociations between arithmetical performance and executive-attentional skills, indicating their functional independence. The analysis at the subject level was also informative with regard to the possible dissociations within the different arithmetical domains. In fact, although almost 40% of the patients were uniformly impaired across tasks and one single patient had a normal general performance, the remaining ones presented profiles characterised by various patterns of preserved/impaired numerical abilities. On the whole, observations at the subject level corroborate numerous findings from investigation of focal brain-damaged patients. Even though, overall, 94% of AD patients showed some form of impairment in number processing and calculation, the patterns of preserved and impaired abilities were extremely different.

Further evidence for an early onset of arithmetical difficulties in AD comes from a study on familial Alzheimer's disease. Kennedy et al. (1995) noticed that the neuropsychological profile of an affected pedigree subject was characterised by an initial memory deficit and early dyscalculia (evaluated by the WAIS-R arithmetic subtest and the Graded Difficulty Arithmetic test, Jackson & Warrington, 1986). Interestingly, numerical skills were reported to be more affected than reading and spelling or even selectively compromised. These findings are not isolated (Nee et al., 1983) and suggest that acalculia may be considered a feature of young-onset or familial AD. Moreover, in the Kennedy et al. study all reported cases showed a cerebral hypometabolism more pronounced in the left temporo-parietal region.

These neuroanatomical considerations were corroborated by an investigation that aimed to identify the cerebral correlates of dyscalculia in minimal and moderate Alzheimer's type dementia. Hirono and collaborators (1998) reported that calculation difficulties, evaluated by means of the WAIS-R arithmetic subtest, correlated significantly with glucose hypometabolism in the left inferior parietal lobule and in the left inferior temporal gyrus. The role of the left inferior parietal lobule in calculation is highly consistent with neuroanatomical evidence from focal brain-damaged patients (see, for a review, Kahn & Whitaker, 1991) and neuroimaging studies in normal subjects (e.g. Dehaene et al., 1999). The involvement of the left inferior temporal gyrus, on the other hand, was interpreted as reflecting the semantic memory requirements, in terms of knowledge of the operations in arithmetic problem solving. Interestingly, although they scored poorly in the WAIS-R arithmetic subtest, most of the patients performed at ceiling on the WAB calculation task. The latter consists of 12 mental arithmetic operations (three for each operation) to which subjects are required to answer orally or by indicating the result among four alternatives. Thus, the observed dissociation may be easily accounted for by the different requirements of the tasks.

BASIC NUMBER SKILLS AND NUMERICAL INFORMATION

The investigation of numerical disorders associated to dementia has mainly concerned numerical transcoding and calculation abilities. However, a few isolated studies have explored more basic numerical competencies, such as counting and numerical comparison. The investigation of these fundamental abilities in demented patients may contribute to clarifying the relationship between these abilities and other arithmetic skills.

In contrast to the attention devoted to the development of these abilities in children (Fuson, 1982, 1988; Gelman & Gallistel, 1978), counting skills have been rarely investigated in neuropsychological studies. The only exception was the study by Seron and collaborators (1991) who analysed dot counting in aphasic patients, right hemisphere lesioned patients, and demented patients. Seron et al. systematically analysed each group's performance both in terms of accuracy and in terms of different counting strategies with reference to four behavioural categories: behaviour referring to the dot pattern (e.g., looking at the dot pattern, pointing to the dot pattern), accompanying behaviour (e.g., oral counting, finger counting), calculation (adding of subclusters already counted), and, finally, transcoding (i.e., use of a different modality or notational system before giving the result in Arabic code). Overall, demented subjects scored significantly lower than both aphasic and right hemisphere patients, showing a mean error rate of 34%. Further, AD patients relied on transcoding strategies more often than the other groups. Oral counting without reference to objects was also assessed. Five out of seven demented subjects counted correctly by threes, three subjects counted by twos, and only two subjects by fives.

The qualitative analysis evidenced continuous manual pointing as the dominant dot-counting behaviour of demented patients; their dominant accompanying behaviour was continuous oral counting. As Seron et al. (1991) suggested, the continuous manual pointing is the least attention-demanding strategy, as each point is named in the simplest and first-acquired number word sequence. All other strategies (such as visual control without pointing, segmented pointing) are more attention-demanding and were mainly used by healthy controls and, to a lesser extent, aphasic and right hemisphere patients; in demented patients these strategies were extremely infrequent.

A recent study by Kaufmann and colleagues (Çano et al., 1998; Kaufmann, & Delazer, 1998) aimed to assess various numerical skills including dot counting and number comparison in mild AD patients. Although AD patients overall were significantly slower than matched controls, their performance was characterised by standard effects systematically observed in these tasks. In dot counting, RTs only marginally increased from two to four dots (with a steep increase of RTs for dot arrays larger than four), thus reflecting the AD patients' preserved ability to subitize small numerosities, i.e., the ability to rapidly recognise small numerosities without counting procedures (Mandler & Shebo, 1982). In number comparison, both AD patients and controls showed a significant split effect, i.e., RTs were faster for pairs of numbers numerically farther apart than for pairs of numbers numerically close. Overall, these results indicate that, in the early stages of AD, basic effects in numerical processing are generally preserved. An analysis at the single-subject level, however, evidenced that few subjects did not show these effects. Most of those patients also presented deficient arithmetical knowledge (e.g., fact and procedural knowledge) but there were exceptions to this rule. Moreover, the opposite pattern has also been observed (namely preserved basic effects and impaired fact and procedural knowledge), thus supporting the double dissociation between basic numerical skills and arithmetic knowledge.

Although numerical knowledge is routinely assessed in arithmetic tasks, this is only one of the multiple contexts where numbers may be encountered. Numbers may also convey non-numerical meanings, as when they are used in labelling context, such as to refer to a specific car model (e.g., Peugeot 506) or to a date (e.g., 1945). This corpus of information includes those numbers that have become "meaningful" by being associated to specific semantic information (e.g., the number 1945 is the end of World War II, and thus it is associated with this event). Recent neuropsychological evidence points to the importance of distinguishing between quantity-based and encyclopaedic number knowledge (e.g., Cohen, Dehaene, & Verstichel, 1994, Delazer & Girelli, 1998), although both may be considered as part of semantic memory. The decline of semantic memory, in particular in the language domain, in AD patients is a well-documented phenomenon (e.g., Hodges, Salmon, & Butters, 1991; Salmon et al., 1988). Recently, demented patients' semantic memory for general facts (i.e., generic knowledge, Nebes, 1989) was investigated by means of the Number Information Test (NIT, Goodglass, Biber, & Freedman, 1984) in a follow-up study carried out by Norton et al. (1997). The test, administered to 142 patients with probable AD of various severities and 78 matched controls, comprises 24 general knowledge questions that require a single number in answer (e.g. "How many days are in a year?"). NIT scores from the AD patients were lower than controls', and mild, moderate, and severe patients all differed between each other, indicating that the test is sensitive to the gradual cognitive decline occurring in AD. Moreover, the high level of consistency on the individual items observed in longitudinal testing favour the hypothesis that, in AD, the deterioration in generic knowledge results from a loss of information rather than from a failure in retrieving it. Interestingly, the NIT and the Boston Naming Test, though highly correlated, independently contributed to discriminate AD patients from controls. This finding led the authors to suggest that the two tests possibly measure different aspects of semantic memory.

NUMBER TRANSCODING

The ability to translate numerals from one code to another is required in numerous daily activities. Despite the apparent easiness of these tasks, multiple independent cognitive mechanisms mediate numerical transcoding. The investigation of the transcoding deficits in demented patients has greatly contributed to the elucidation of the modular structure of these mechanisms, the impairment of which may be highly selective and give rise to a very specific error pattern.

Noël and Seron (1995) described a 71-year-old patient, LR, suffering from probable Alzheimer's type dementia. LR complained of progressive difficulties in dealing with numbers, for instance in daily-life situations requiring the manipulation of money. From the evaluation of his numerical abilities emerged a difficulty in writing Arabic numerals characterised by a particular error pattern. Errors were of the syntactic type and frequently consisted in literal transcriptions of the verbal word forms (e.g., *mille quatre cents* [one thousand four hundred] ⟶ 1000400). The qualitative analysis of LR's error pattern indicated that product relationships (e.g., two thousand ⟶ [2 × 1000]) were better mastered than sum relationships (e.g., one thousand four hundred ⟶ [1000 + 400]) (Power & Longuet-Higgins, 1990). The authors argued that this specific error pattern could hardly be explained within a base-ten production system such as the one depicted by McCloskey (e.g., McCloskey, Caramazza, & Basili, 1985). By contrast, these results favour a production model that postulates number semantic representation reflecting the structure of the verbal numeral (e.g., Power & Dal Martello, 1990).

A further case study by Noël and Seron (1993) described NR, with probable Alzheimer's type dementia, who showed a specific deficit in reading Arabic numerals. The patient's reading error pattern and his performance in several number-processing tasks allowed the authors to locate the deficit in the syntactic module of the Arabic comprehension system. Moreover, it was observed that judgements in semantic tasks, such as number comparison, were based on intact semantic processing, based on the expected and incorrect verbal transcoded forms, e.g., 236 was read as 2306 and judged superior to 1258. Noël and Seron (1993) interpreted this finding as evidence for semantic transcoding routes as postulated in McCloskey's model. Further, they proposed a preferred entry code hypothesis which postulates that the access to number semantic representations may be accomplished either from the verbal or the Arabic code, according to the individual's idiosyncratic preference for maintaining the information in working memory in an auditory or a visual code. In the specific case of NR, it was assumed that the verbal form constituted the preferred code to access semantics; however, as the verbal forms were based on incorrect syntactic processing, the patient's performance was characterised by the observed error pattern.

The analysis of impaired number processing in demented patients constituted the basis for the development of a number-processing model proposed by Cipolotti and Butterworth (1995). In particular, patient SF, a 52-year-old bank manager suffering from Alzheimer's disease, showed a selective deficit in reading aloud Arabic numerals in the absence of comprehension and production problems. In fact, he could answer questions concerning numerical knowledge and cognitive estimations correctly in verbal form, but frequently failed to read Arabic numerals (Cipolotti, 1995). Similarly, patient SAM (Cipolotti & Butterworth, 1995), a 57-year-old chemist suffering from a progressive degenerative condition of unknown origin, presented a dissociation between impaired verbal and Arabic numeral production in transcoding tasks and preserved spoken and Arabic numeral production in calculation tasks. Thus, in both cases, the observed difficulties producing a particular number code were task-specific. On the basis of these results the authors suggested a multiple routes model for number processing. They proposed that numeral output systems can be accessed not only via abstract semantic representations, but also through asemantic routes that bypass the abstract internal representation. Furthermore, they postulated dedicated control mechanisms that, on the basis of task requirements, would select one specific route and inhibit the others.

The evaluation of transcoding skills in groups of demented patients has mainly entailed the administration of tasks with null or minimal memory requirements, such as tasks of written transcoding.

In 1990 Tegner and Nyback studied the transcoding from Arabic to written verbal numerals in a group of Alzheimer patients. They found characteristic intrusions of the Arabic code into the alphabetic code (e.g., 43 ⟶ fyrtio3 [fourty3]), an error type never reported in normal subjects and aphasic patients. The authors attributed the intrusions to a failure to suppress the more automatised behaviour of using Arabic numerals compared to verbal numerals. However, this explanation would be inadequate to account for the reverse pattern of errors, i.e., intrusions from the verbal code into the Arabic one. This evidence has recently been reported by Kessler and Kalbe (1996) who studied transcoding from verbal numerals into Arabic numerals and vice versa in a group of patients with probable Alzheimer's disease. The results indicated frequent transcoding errors in both tasks and, in particular, intrusions of elements of the source code in the target code, e.g., 3436 ⟶ 3tausendvierhundert36 (3thousandfourhundred36). These errors were interpreted as the result of temporary failure of the control mechanisms in a multiple impaired cognitive system. However, as pointed out by Thioux et al. (1999), a deficit in the supervisory attentional system *per se* may not explain a unidirectional pattern of intrusion errors such as the one they observed. Thioux and colleagues systematically investigated this phenomenon in a single-case study. They described a patient suffering from Alzheimer's disease who showed a specific deficit in the production of Arabic numerals. In particular, most of the errors produced consisted in intrusions of the verbal code into the Arabic one (e.g., *3 mille* instead of 3000 [trois mille]). Interestingly, the proportion of shift errors was modulated by the extent to which a task was tied to the Arabic code (e.g., written calculation is strongly associated to the Arabic code; delayed copy of Arabic numerals, on the other hand, may induce verbal storage of the stimuli) and by the familiarity of the tasks, with less familiar tasks being more prone to interference. The analysis of the patient's performance at different stages of the disease disclosed a progressive disappearance of the Arabic code from the patient's written production. The attempt to classify the errors in different categories and the comparison of the patient's performance in various tasks suggested the presence of two deficits: a transcoding-specific difficulty in activating the Arabic form of numerals on the one hand, and a more general impairment of inhibitory processes on the other hand.

Further evidence against a mere attentional interpretation of the intrusion errors comes from a study by Gentileschi et al. (1998). In the attempt to compare the occurrence of transcoding errors in healthy subjects (n = 140), aphasic (n = 8) and demented patients (n = 20), they observed that code-intrusion errors characterised the transcoding performance of the latter group only. However, at the individual level, the observation of AD patients who do not produce intrusions, as well as the lack of correlation between severity of the disease and incidence of intrusions, cast doubts on an interpretation in terms of attentional deficit only.

CALCULATION PROCESSES

It is well established that calculation skills include a number of different competencies, among which are the retrieval of arithmetic. facts, and knowledge and execution of arithmetic procedures. Evidence from dementia supports the functional independence of these distinct abilities but also the multiple mechanisms mediating each of them.

The first systematic report of calculation disorders in dementia has been provided by Grafman et al. (1989). They described the case of a retired army general with progressive dementia whose initial complaint was dyscalculia. The authors studied the patient's calculation abilities and number processing over 2 years until he was unable even to recognise and discriminate numbers. The initial impairment was limited to multiplication facts and to multiplication and division procedures, yet the longitudinal examination showed a decline in all calculation tasks. Magnitude comparison and number knowledge, on the other hand, were intact even when other arithmetic knowledge and calculation abilities were grossly impaired.

Whereas Grafman et al.'s patient showed, at the early stage of the disease, a selective deficit in calculation in the context of preserved language abilities, Diesfeldt (1993) described a demented patient with the opposite pattern. Despite severe language problems (such as difficulties in word retrieval and comprehension), the patient performed simple additions and subtractions within the normal range and showed only minor difficulties in multiplication. Over the course of 18 months, his arithmetic facts knowledge progressively deteriorated and the patient had often to rely on back-up strategies to solve even the simplest calculation. On the other hand, his performance in written calculation indicated mastery of calculation procedures, all errors being determined by a failure in fact retrieval. In an attempt to draw parallels between the language deterioration and the calculation decline, Diesfield suggested that, in both domains, the patient's difficulties were limited to the retrieval of stored semantic information (arithmetic facts and lexical items) while procedural knowledge was preserved (syntax and arithmetic algorithms). Diesfield proposed two independent brain systems, one dedicated to the storage of the semantic memory traces, the other dedicated to the rule-governed processes of language and calculation. Within this framework, his patient's deficit resulted from a selective deterioration to the former system.

In a further follow-up study Girelli et al. (1999) reported the progressive dissolution of numerical skills in EP, a former teacher of mathematics, suffering from an Alzheimer's type dementia. The longitudinal examination revealed a pattern of decline different from previous reported cases. At the very early stage of her illness, EP was fast and accurate in performing a wide range of transcoding and calculation tasks. Among the latter, she could easily answer any arithmetical fact and two-digit mental calculation. However, when required to solve written calculation, she showed some difficulties with the borrowing procedure in subtraction and was severely impaired in the application of the multiplication algorithm. One year later, her performance in written calculation indicated increasing difficulties in the execution of arithmetical procedures, although minor difficulties also emerged in mental addition and subtraction and in a number composition task. In a further evaluation, 18 months after onset, her numerical skills were severely compromised and her difficulties extended to estimation tasks, number composition, and, to a lesser extent, transcoding tasks. Yet, within arithmetical facts, her knowledge of multiplication tables was relatively preserved. Thus, an initial impairment in arithmetical procedures was followed by an insidious decay in more basic numerical tasks with a selective preservation of arithmetical facts. This investigation confirmed the functional independence of facts and procedures within the calculation system, and suggests that, in the context of a general cognitive decline, specific numerical skills may be more resistant to deterioration.

Further evidence for the functional architecture of the calculation system comes from a study by Pesenti and collaborators (Pesenti, Seron, & Van der Linden, 1994). They investigated the arithmetical difficulties shown by patient BB, a 39-year-old woman suffering from a precocious evolving dementia. As compared to other cognitive domains, BB experienced particular difficulties in calculation. Within simple arithmetic, she showed an interesting dissociation between severely impaired multiplication, moderately impaired addition, and significantly better preserved subtraction. This dissociation was evident in production as well as in verification tasks. Moreover, she showed a dissociation between problems which can be answered by a stored rule (e.g., $n \times 1$) and other problems (e.g., 2×3), the former being better mastered. Thus, this case supports not only the modular composition of the calculation system, but also, as argued by the authors, the segregated storage of different arithmetic operations.

Calculation abilities in patients suffering from Alzheimer's type dementia ($n = 23$) and patients with vascular dementia ($n = 19$) were tested in a study by Marterer et al. (1996). The performance in addition and multiplication problems was systematically lower in both AD groups than controls and was found to correlate with the severity of the disease. However, the attempt to analyse the performance qualitatively did not prove to be useful in the differential diagnosis of dementia.

A recent group study by Mantovan et al. (1999) investigated the breakdown of calculation procedures in patients affected by Alzheimer's disease. In this study AD patients at an early stage of the disease had particular difficulties in performing complex calculation procedures as compared to the retrieval of arithmetic facts. A qualitative analysis of procedural errors revealed clear differences between the systematic errors reported in both developmental studies and acquired dyscalculia (Girelli & Delazer, 1996) on the one hand, and AD patients' errors on the other hand. A subject-by-subject analysis showed a low consistency across problems and a high variability of errors. Further, errors appeared more frequently at the end of the procedure. Moreover, AD patients frequently perseverated on erroneous steps in the procedure and rarely used prompts provided by the examiner, thus showing low awareness of their deficits. Overall, the qualitative analysis indicates that AD patients' poor performance with calculation procedures is grounded in difficulties in the execution and monitoring of a complex algorithm, but less in difficulties in retrieving from long-term memory the underlying algorithm itself (Semenza, Miceli, & Girelli, 1997). Indeed, the execution of calculation procedures is a multi-step process involving different types of cognitive resources. In fact, different cognitive tasks (e.g., writing, memorising, planning) have to be performed concurrently, which may present major difficulties to AD patients (Baddeley et al., 1986; Becker, 1988; Grober & Sliwinski, 1991).

In the study by Kaufmann & Delazer (1998), AD patients were administered multiple calculation tasks. In simple arithmetic, AD patients performed addition and multiplication flawlessly, while they scored significantly lower than controls in subtraction and division. AD patients also showed particular difficulties with problems that are supposed to be answered by a stored rule (e.g., $n \times 0 = 0$). In line with other studies (Grafman et al., 1989; Mantovan et al., 1999), AD patients showed multiple difficulties with arithmetical procedures. A qualitative error analysis revealed various error types, including incomplete operations, failures in the selection of factors, and also distorted calculation algorithms. A few specific error tendencies (like full-naming errors, operand-intrusion errors, perseverations), which were even more frequent at a 1-year follow-up examination, are compatible with the hypothesis of deficient monitoring mechanisms and deficient inhibitory control (Mantovan et al., 1999; Semenza et al., 1997).

SELECTIVE PRESERVATION OF CALCULATION SKILLS IN DEMENTIA

Although evidence so far indicates that numerical disorders may well be considered part of the cognitive decline occurring in dementia, two single-case studies of selective preservation of calculation abilities in otherwise cognitively impaired demented patients have been reported.

Remond-Besuchet et al. (1999) described the case of an 86-year-old patient affected by dementia of mild severity who, despite presenting impairment in several cognitive domains, had an extraordinary preserved competence in computing mental multi-digit multiplications and square roots. His cognitive deterioration extended to language, memory, reasoning, and praxis functions. Interestingly, he showed a rather heterogeneous performance within the numerical domain as well. His knowledge of number magnitude and parity status was preserved, although he failed in a Piagetian conservation task. Within simple arithmetic, intact arithmetical facts knowledge dissociated from defective knowledge of arithmetical rules (e.g., $N \times 0 = 0$). Moreover, arithmetical procedures were only partially preserved, with the multiplication algorithm being completely compromised. Beside this irregular performance across numerical tests, the patient answered multiplication and division tables as well and as fast as young controls and mastered, well above average, mental multi-digit multiplication in terms of both speed and accuracy. Further, he was clearly superior to any young and highly educated control subject in square recognition and root extraction, even of large numbers. From the analysis of the patient's performance the authors concluded that an extended semantic memory for arithmetical facts and a reliable procedural knowledge of compensatory solution algorithms were both responsible for the patient's exceptional, but rather limited, calculation abilities. Yet, from the patient's own declaration as well as from his overall cognitive profile, the authors interpreted the case as an example of better resistance of overlearned functions rather than of a selective preservation of exceptional abilities.

A further case of preservation of calculation abilities in AD was reported by McGlinchey-Berroth, Milberg, and Charness (1989). This study investigated the residual learning skills in an 82-year-old demented patient who, despite severe amnesia, preserved his above-average premorbid proficiency in basic arithmetic. This fact allowed the authors to test the patient's ability to learn a rather complex algorithm to square two-digit numbers. By comparing his overall performance with his performance in executing the individual steps of the algorithm, it was concluded that the patient's improvement was determined only by his increasing efficiency in computing the single steps. These latter mainly consisted in addition, subtraction, and multiplication, the computation of which required well-preserved mental calculation abilities. Yet he remained relatively unable to consolidate these steps in a single algorithm. The authors suggest that AD-reduced learning abilities may be determined by a deficit in combining the individual steps of a procedure.

DISCUSSION

Overall, converging evidence from both group studies (Deloche et al., 1995; Parlato et al., 1992) and single-case studies (Grafman et al., 1989; Pesenti et al., 1994) suggests that numerical disorders should be included among the early signs of AD.

Different prevalence of arithmetical disorders in AD across studies may be simply explained by the different inclusion criteria adopted. Similarly, contrasting patterns of correlation between numerical performance and other cognitive functions (language, memory, etc.) may be attributed to major methodological differences across studies, i.e., the different type of numerical and non-numerical tasks adopted.

Further, it seems plausible to conclude that, at an early stage of AD, deficits in the numerical domain may occur independently from deficits in other cognitive functions (Deloche, 1995). One may suggest that calculation and number-processing mechanisms, being highly specific and acquired later in development, constitute a rather difficult and unsteady domain of knowledge compared to others, and thus are more sensitive to cerebral damage. However, preserved numerical abilities have been observed, though less frequently, in patients with impaired memory (McGlinchey-Berroth et al., 1989) or language disorders (Diesfeldt, 1993). Indeed, the selective preservation of remarkable calculation skills in an otherwise deteriorated cognitive patient has recently been documented (e.g., Remond-Besuchet et al., 1999). Thus, difficulty and/or complexity effects may not adequately account for the selective numerical disorders frequently observed in the early stages of AD. More appropriate seems the conclusion that number-processing and calculation abilities are functionally independent from other cognitive abilities, allowing patterns of selective deficit or preservation.

The pattern of preserved and impaired numerical abilities may differ greatly across AD patients. Group studies seem to indicate that, even at an early stage of the illness, all aspects of number skills are frequently affected; yet, more selective impairments to one specific processing mechanism or system may also occur. At the early stage of AD, selective deficits in number processing have been reported and, in several cases, they involved highly specific mechanisms within the transcoding processes (Cipolotti, 1995; Cipolotti & Butterworth, 1995; Noël & Seron, 1993). Interestingly, although different types of errors have been observed according to the specific functional impairment, the systematic analysis of disturbed performance has allowed the identification of typical transcoding errors in AD patients' performance (Kessler & Kalbe, 1996; Tegner & Nyback, 1990). These cross-code intrusions are likely to be determined by the co-occurence of a specific transcoding deficit and a more general decline in inhibitory mechanisms (Thioux et al., 1999).

Lack of or inefficient executive control also seems to play a role in the frequent difficulties AD patients experience with arithmetic procedures. Again, both group studies (e.g. Kaufman & Delazer, 1998; Mantovan et al., 1999) and single-case follow-ups (Girelli et al., 1999; Grafman et al., 1989) reported procedural calculation deficits as an early sign of Alzheimer's disease. Again, the qualitative analyses of the patients' performance indicate a variety of errors, among which many result from deficient monitoring and inhibitory mechanisms. Yet, within calculation abilities, selective deficits in arithmetic facts knowledge have also been observed. Moreover a case of preserved subtraction and disturbed addition and multiplication facts has been documented (Pesenti et al., 1994) as well as a deficit limited to multiplication facts (Diesfeldt, 1993).

Clearly any attempt to provide a standard pattern of decline of numerical abilities in AD is simply pointless. Even when group studies seemed to identify some general trends, the observation at the single subject level always disclosed high variability between individual performances, often revealing double dissociations of theoretical importance.

In summary, various and highly specific numerical disorders may emerge in AD. At an early stage, deficits may be limited either to transcoding abilities or to calculation abilities; in both cases they may involve very selective mechanisms or subcomponents.

Although, at the general level, the multiple difficulties showed by AD patients may be quantitatively and qualitatively similar to the numerical disorders determined by cerebral focal lesions, few typical error patterns may differentially identify dyscalculia in dementia.

Taken together, the evidence discussed in the present review suggests that numerical deficits should be considered among the early signs of AD. This conclusion urges the inclusion of a numerical assessment in diagnostic batteries for AD and possibly the development of effective intervention for helping patients to overcome the daily difficulties in number processing.

REFERENCES

Baddeley, A.D., Logie, R.H., Bressi, S., Della Sala, S., & Spinnler, H. (1986). Dementia and working memory. *Quarterly Journal of Experimental Psychology*, *38*, 603-618.

Becker, J.T. (1988). Working memory and secondary memory deficits in Alzheimer's Disease. *Journal of Clinical and Experimental Neuropsychology*, *10*, 739–753.

Cano, C., Kaufmann, L., Montanes, P., Jaquier, M., Matallana, D., & Delazer, M. (1998). *Dot estimation, number comparison and arithmetic in Alzheimer patients*. Poster presented at the 6th International Conference on Alzheimer's Disease, Amsterdam.

Carlomagno, S., Iavarone, A., Nolfe, G., Bourene G., Martin, C., & Deloche, G. (1999). Dyscalculia in the early stages of Alzhemier's disease. *Acta Neurologica Scandinava*, *99*, 166–174.

Cipolotti, L. (1995). Multiple routes for reading words, why not numbers? Evidence from a case of Arabic numeral dyslexia. *Cognitive Neuropsychology*, *12*, 313–362.

Cipolotti, L., & Butterworth, B. (1995). Toward a multiroute model of number processing: Impaired transcoding with preserved calculation skills. *Journal of Experimental Psychology: General*, *124*(4), 375–390.

Cohen, L., Dehaene, S., & Verstichel, P. (1994). Number words and number non-words. A case of deep dyslexia extending to Arabic numerals. *Brain*, *117*, 267–279.

Dagenbach, D., & McCloskey, M. (1992). The organisation of arithmetic facts in memory: Evidence from a brain-damaged patient. *Brain and Cognition*, *20*, 345–366.

Dehaene, S., Spelke, E., Pinel, P., Stanescu, R., & Tsivkin, S. (1999). Sources of mathematical thinking: Behavioral and brain-imaging evidence. *Science*, *284*, 970–974.

Delazer, M., & Girelli, L. (1998). When "Alfa Romeo' facilitates '164': Semantic effects in verbal number production. *Neurocase*, *3*(6), 461–475.

Deloche, G., Hannequin, D., Carlomagno, S., Angiel, A., Dordain, M., Pasquier, F., Pellat, J., Denis, P., Desi, M., Beauchamp, D., Metz-Lutz, M.N., Cesaro, P., & Seron, X. (1995). Calculation and number processing in mild Alzheimer's disease. *Journal of Clinical and Experimental Neuropsychology*, *17*, 634–639.

Deloche, G., Seron, X., Larroque, C., Magnien, C., Metz-Lutz, C., Noël, M.N., Riva, I., Schils, J.P., Dordain, M., Ferrand, I., Baeta, E., Basso, A., Cipolotti, L., Claros-Salinas, D., Horward, D., Gaillard, F., Golderberg, G., Mazzucchi, A., Stachowiak, F., Tzavaras, A., Vendrell, J., Bergego, C., & Pradat-Diehl, P. (1994). Calculation and number processing: Assessment battery; Role of demographic factors. *Journal of Clinical and Experimental Neuropsychology*, *16*, 195–208.

Diesfeldt, H. (1993). Progressive decline of semantic memory with preservation of number processing and calculation. *Behavioural Neurology*, *6*, 239–242.

Fuson, K.C. (1982). An analysis of the counting-on solution procedure in addition. In Th.P. Carpenter, J.M. Moser, & Th.A. Romberg (Eds.), *Addition and subtraction: A cognitive perspective*. Hillsdale, NJ: Lawrence Erlbaum Associates Inc.

Fuson, K.C. (1988). *Children's counting and concepts of number*. New York: Springer.

Gelman, R., & Gallistel, C.R. (1978). *The child's understanding of number*. Cambridge, MA: Harvard University Press.

Gentileschi, V., Della Sala, S., Gray, C., & Spinnler, H. (1998). *Transcoding errors in patients with Alzheimer's disease and aphasia*. Poster presented at the 16th European Workshop on Cognitive Neurpsychology, Bressanone, Italy.

Girelli, L., & Delazer, M. (1996). Subtraction bugs in an acalculic patient. *Cortex*, *32*, 547–555.

Girelli, L., Luzzatti, C., Annoni, G., & Vecchi, T. (1999). Progressive decline of numerical skills in Alzheimer-type dementia: A case study. *Brain and Cognition*, *40*, 132–136.

Goodglass, H., Biber, C., & Freedman, M. (1984). *Memory factors in naming disorders in aphasics and*

Alzheimer patients. Paper presented at the Annual Conference of the International Neuropsychological Society, Houston, Texas.

Grafman, J., Kampen, D., Rosemberg, J., Salazar, A.M., & Boller, F. (1989). The progressive breakdown of number processing and calculation ability: A case study. *Cortex, 25*, 121–133.

Grober, E., & Sliwinski, M.J. (1991). Dual-task performance in demented and nondemented elderly. *Journal of Clinical and Experimental Neuropsychology, 13*, 667–676.

Hirono, N., Mori, E., Ishii, K., Imamura, T., Shimomura, T., Tanimukai, S., Kazui, H., Hashimoto, M., Yamashita, H., & Sasaki, M. (1998). Regional metabolism: Associations with dyscalculia in Alzheimer's disease. *Journal of Neurology, Neurosurgery and Psychiatry, 65*, 913–916.

Hodges, J.R., Salmon, D.P., & Butters, N. (1991). The nature of the naming deficit in Alzheimer's disease. *Brain, 114*, 1547–1558.

Jackson, M., & Warrington, E.K. (1986). Arithmetic skills in patients with unilateral cerebral lesions. *Cortex, 22*, 611–620.

Kahn, H., & Whitaker, H.A. (1991). Acalculia: An historical review of localization. *Brain and Cognition, 17*, 102–115.

Kaufmann, L., & Delazer, M. (1998). *Number comparison, dot counting and arithmetic in Alzheimer patients*. 16th European Workshop on Cognitive Neuropsychology, Bressanone, Italy.

Kennedy, A.M., Newman, S.K., Frackowiak, R.S.J., Cunningham, V.J., Roques, P., Stevens, J., Nearly, D., Bruton, C.J., Warrington, E.K., & Rossor, M.N. (1995). Chromosome 14 linked familial Alzheimer's disease. A clinico-pathological study of a single pedigree. *Brain, 118*, 185–205.

Kessler, J., & Kalbe, E. (1996). Written numeral transcoding in patients with Alzheimer's disease. *Cortex, 32*, 755–761.

Mandler, G., & Shebo, B.J. (1982). Subitizing: An analysis of its component processes. *Journal of Experimental Psychology: General, 11*, 1–22.

Mantovan, C., Delazer, M., Ermani, M., & Denes, G. (1999). The breakdown of calculation procedures in Alzheimer's disease. *Cortex, 35*, 21–38.

Marterer, A., Danielczyk, W., Simanyi, M., & Fischer, P. (1996). Calculation abilities in dementia of Alzheimer's type and in vascular dementia. *Archives of Gerontology Geriatrics, 23*(2), 189–197.

McCloskey, M., Caramazza, A., & Basili, A. (1985). A cognitive mechanism in number processing and calculation: Evidence from dyscalculia. *Brain and Cognition, 4*, 171–196.

McGlinchey-Berrot, R., Milberg, W.P., & Charness, N. (1989). Learning of a complex arithmetic skill in dementia: Further evidence for a dissociation between compilation and production. *Cortex, 25*, 697–705.

Nebes, R.D. (1989). Semantic memory in Alzheimer's disease. *Psychological Bulletin, 106*, 377–394.

Nee, L.E., Polinsky R.J., Elridge, R., Weingartner, H., Smallberg, S., & Ebert, M. (1983). A family with histologically confirmed Alzheimer's disease. *Archives of Neurology, 40*, 203–208.

Noël, M.P., & Seron, X. (1993). Arabic number reading deficit: A single-case study or when 236 is read (2306) and judged superior to 1258. *Cognitive Neuropsychology, 10*, 317–339.

Noël, M.P., & Seron, X. (1995). Lexicalization errors in writing Arabic numerals: A single case study. *Brain and Cognition, 29*, 151–179.

Norton, L.E., Bondi, M.K., Salmon, D.P., & Goodglass, H. (1997). Deterioration of generic knowledge in patients with Alzheimer's disease: Evidence from the number information test. *Journal of Clinical and Experimental Neuropsychology, 19*(6), 857–866.

Parlato, V., Lopez, O.L., Panisset, M., Iavarone, A., Grafman, F., & Boller, F. (1992). Mental calculation in mild Alzheimer's disease: A pilot study. *International Journal of Geriatric Psychiatry, 7*, 599–602.

Pesenti, M., Seron, X., & Van der Linden, M. (1994). Selective impairment as evidence for mental organisation of arithmetical facts: BB, a case of preserved subtraction? *Cortex, 30*, 661–671.

Power, R.J.D., & Dal Martello, M.F. (1990). The dictation of Italian numerals. *Language and Cognitive Processes, 5*, 237–254.

Power, R.J.D., & Longuet-Higgins, H.C. (1978). Learning to count: A computational model of language acquisition. *Proceedings of the Royal Society of London, B, 200*, 391–417.

Remond-Besuchet, C., Noël, M.-P., Seron, X., Thioux, M., Brun, M., & Aspe, X. (1999). Selective preservation of exceptional arithmetical knowledge in a demented patient. *Mathematical Cognition, 5*(1), 41–64.

Salmon, D.P., Shimamura, A.P., Butters, N., & Smith, S. (1988). Lexical and semantic deficits in patients with Alzheimer's disease. *Journal of Clinical and Experimental Neuropsychology, 10*, 477–494.

Semenza, C., Miceli, L., & Girelli, L. (1997). A deficit for arithmetical procedures: Lack of knowledge or lack of monitoring? *Cortex, 33*, 483–498.

Seron, X., Deloche, G., Ferrand, I., Cornet, J.A., Frederix, M., & Hirsbrunner, T. (1991). Dot counting by brain damaged subjects. *Brain and Cognition, 17*, 116–137.

Tegner, R., & Nyback, H. (1990). 'Two hundred and twenty 4our': A study of transcoding in dementia. *Acta Neurologica Scandinavica, 81,* 177–178.

Thioux, M., Seron, X., Turconi, E., & Ivanoiu, A. (1999). Intrusion of the verbal code during the production of Arabic numerals: A single case study in a patient with probable Alzheimer's disease. *Cognitive Neuropsychology, 16,* 749–773.

APHASIOLOGY, 2001, *15* (7), 695–712

Rehabilitation of number processing and calculation skills

Luisa Girelli

Università degli Studi di Milano-Bicocca, Milan, Italy

Xavier Seron

Université Catholique de Louvain, Belgium

The main purpose of this article is to present the research that has been done on the rehabilitation of number and calculation disorders. It is argued that theoretically based rehabilitation of arithmetical processing requires the formulation of a detailed functional diagnosis based on a theoretically driven evaluation of numerical processing and calculation skills. Up to now, the strategies that have been adopted in this rehabilitation field have mainly consisted in attempts to re-teach lost knowledge via extensive practice. These therapeutic programmes are described in two domains: the transcoding of numerals and the retrieval of arithmetical facts. Finally, the authors underline the necessity to develop in the near future programmes of rehabilitation adopting a more ecological perspective.

INTRODUCTION

The importance of numbers in daily life is largely underestimated. Numbers are used in countless everyday activities and in many different contexts. We use numbers to do our shopping, to verify our bank account, to pay bills, to control our weight, to adjust the speed of our car, to be on time for an appointment, etc. Numbers are also used to order various things in our surroundings (houses in a street, offices, or floors in a building), and to label or to identify different exemplars in a category of things such as telephone users, car models, county departments, city districts. Not only are we continuously exposed to numbers, we are also required to recognise, understand, or produce; but we are frequently obliged to manipulate them to do some basic operations such as quantity comparisons or calculations. Dealing with money is one of the more frequent and familiar situations that tap our mathematical skills; but there are many other activities that require number manipulation such as time estimation, cooking, do-it-yourself activities, games, needlework, sports, architecture, engineering, science, and so on.

Thus it seems surprising that we are so little aware of the functional importance of our numerical and arithmetical skills. This partial neglect is probably due to the fact that, for an educated adult, basic mathematical skills represent overlearned and almost automatic processes. However, if for any reason, this acquired competence is no longer reliable, it

Address correspondence to: Luisa Girelli, Università degli Studi di Milano-Bicocca, Dipartimento di Psicologia, Edifico U6, Piazza del' Ateneo Nuovo 1, 20126 Milano, Italia. Email: luisa.girelli@unimib.it

The first author was supported by a Wellcome Grant n. 054721.

http://www.tandf.co.uk/journals/pp/02687038.html   DOI:10.1080/02687040143000131

results in an important deficit which extends to many different daily-life activities[1]. So it is not misleading to think that a lack of numeracy skills is equally as handicapping as illiteracy.

Unfortunately, numerical skills are highly sensitive to brain injury. The inability to deal with numbers and to calculate is a frequent result of brain damage: according to Jackson and Warrington (1986), almost 10% of patients with left hemisphere lesion show a selective deficit in arithmetic, and more than 90% of patients with Alzheimer's disease at the early stage present some mathematical deficits (Carlomagno et al., 1999). Mathematical deficits are also frequently associated with language deficits (Dahmen et al., 1982; Delazer et al., 1999; Hécaen, & Houiller, 1961). Thus, the increasing interest in the study of mathematical disorders subsequent to a brain lesion is certainly justified.

In the last 30 years, neuropsychology has played a crucial role in elucidating some of the cognitive mechanisms underlying mathematical skills. It is now well established that mathematical skills can be fractionated into functionally independent components, some of which are considered as distinct from other cognitive functions such as language (Rossor, Warrington, & Cipolotti, 1995; Thioux et al., 1998) and memory (Butterworth, Cipolotti, & Warrington, 1995). Moreover, several systematic single-case studies proved that both numerical processing and calculation are complex multi-component cognitive functions, all of which may be selectively impaired (for a review, see Butterworth, 1999; McCloskey, 1992; Pesenti & Seron, 2000).

Therefore, the classical acalculia syndromes such as spatial and verbal acalculias and anarithmetia (Hécaen et al., 1961) appear to be unable to describe the diversity of the arithmetical disorders, although these taxonomies rightly point to the existence of different mathematical deficits and to the presence of frequently associated disorders. For this reason, too, the rehabilitation of arithmetical disorders cannot be based on their traditional classification, but requires the formulation of a detailed functional diagnosis based on a theoretically driven evaluation of the patient's numerical processing and calculation skills. However, despite the continuous refinement of cognitive models in the domain of arithmetic cognition, up to now very little effort has been directed to the development of efficient rehabilitation programmes. The lack of concerted effort in the rehabilitation of numerical disorders is well reflected in the paucity of existing contributions as well as in their pioneering approach.

Concerning the strategies adopted in this rehabilitation field, the treatment of mathematical deficits mostly consists in attempts to re-teach lost knowledge via extensive practice, the underlying assumption being that practising would restore the functionality of the impaired component. Thus, for example, a patient with a specific deficit in the retrieval of arithmetical facts would undergo frequent and controlled drills with the problems he or she can no longer answer, until the association between problem and correct answer was re-established (Miceli, Capasso, & Temusi, 1987).

Because of the long-lasting and structured learning process by which numerical skills are acquired across development, the re-education of numerical deficits may indeed require the use of some distinctive procedures. For the sake of clarity, let us consider just one example. The mastery of simple arithmetic is characterised by accurate and fast performance in the solution of single-digit operations. It is assumed that when presented with a simple operation, such as "5×4", normal adults quickly retrieve the solution

---

[1] Neglect of calculation disorders is even more evident in developmental neuropsychology, while incidence of dyscalculia in children varies between 3.6% and 6% according to the research (Kosc, 1974; Lewis, Hitch, & Walker, 1994)

from long-term memory storage, bypassing any on-line calculation procedure (for a review, see Ashcraft, 1992). However, this competence is achieved through a long and effortful learning process during which children apply back-up strategies and procedural methods to solve simple operations[2]. When the ability to access or retrieve arithmetical facts knowledge is compromised after a cerebral lesion, the rehabilitative intervention may adopt two different approaches. First, extensive practice may be promoted in order to re-learn the facts or re-automatise the retrieval process; second, efficient back-up strategies based on the patient's residual skills (e.g., counting-on procedures: 6×4 by $6 + 6 + 6 + 6$; decomposition strategies: $7 + 8$ by $7 + 3 = 10 + 5 = 15$) may be systematically taught to compute the solution of any unknown problem. Even if those indirect approaches induce a qualitatively different behaviour from the pre-morbid one, the main objective of the therapy, i.e., to enable the patient to rely on his or her computation ability, is equally achieved. Moreover, the systematic use of reconstructive strategies does eventually lead to re-learning the facts. Thus, to some extent, the development of specific remedial techniques in calculation rehabilitation may benefit from what we know about the processing mechanisms that facilitate the acquisition of calculation skills during development.

So far, very few studies have been devoted to the rehabilitation of numerical skills, and the existing contributions mainly focus on two distinct abilities: numerical transcoding and calculation. The former refers to the ability to translate numerical stimuli from one code to a different one (e.g., 4 $\longrightarrow$ four), while calculation includes both knowledge of simple arithmetical facts and knowledge of arithmetical procedures required to solve multi-digit calculation. Attention has also been given to the rehabilitation of arithmetical-word problem solving (e.g., Delazer, Bodner, & Benke, 1998; Fasotti, Bremer, & Eling, 1992). Even though these studies concern the remediation of the encoding processes rather than the executive aspects of arithmetical problem solving, their contribution is certainly worthwhile.

REHABILITATION OF TRANSCODING ACTIVITIES

In everyday situations we are frequently confronted with the processing of numbers presented in different codes. More frequently numbers are presented in the verbal code in auditory modality or in the Arabic code in the written modality[3]. Processing of numerals thus implies the mastery of two different codes as well as the ability to pass from one code to the other, i.e., what is called transcoding activities. To restrict the analysis to the two most used codes and the two modalities of presentation, six main transcoding activities may be considered (see Figure 1).

The Arabic code has a restricted lexicon of 10 digits 0,1,2 ... 9 which represents the integers smaller than the base. It is a positional notation system, into which each digit in the numeral determines the power of the base by which it must be multiplied. When a position in the base is empty it is filled by a "0". The verbal system is more complex. The lexicon is composed of different classes: units (from one to nine), ten (from ten to ninety) and teens (from eleven to nineteen) and words that represent some powers of the base such as hundred, thousand, million.

---

[2] There is a clear paucity of studies devoted to calculation disorders compared to the many studies on developmental dyslexia.

[3] There are of course more than two different codes for representing quantities, such as Roman code or the binary code, but these codes are used less frequently and in more restricted contexts.

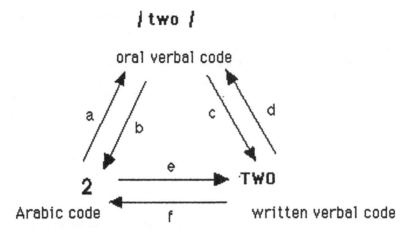

/ two /

oral verbal code

a
b
c
d

e
2 ⟶ TWO

Arabic code   f   written verbal code

a : reading aloud an Arabic numeral
b : writing down under dictation of an Arabic numeral
c : writing down under dictation of a written verbal numeral
d : reading aloud a written verbal numeral
e : writing down a verbal numeral from an Arabic numeral
f ; writing down an Arabic numeral from a written verbal numeral

Figure 1. The six main numeral transcoding tasks.

From case to case, one or more than one transcoding activity may be impaired. The errors may be of a lexical or a syntactical nature: lexical errors concern one element of the numeral (74 transcoded as *sixty* four) whereas syntactical errors concern the syntactic structure of the numeral and result in numerals that generally have an incorrect magnitude (72 transcoded as *seven hundred and two* or *three thousand and forty nine* transcoded as 3000409).

The first rehabilitation studies on numerical transcoding disorders were done with reference to the asemantic model proposed by Deloche and Seron (1987) which specifies the algorithm and rules mediating the transcoding processes. The treatment followed a "reconstitution of function" rationale, which consisted in a step by step re-teaching of explicit transcoding rules. A first study by Deloche, Seron, and Ferrand (1989) was devoted to two aphasic patients both at a chronic stage of their illness. The first one, a 42-year-old man, suffered from a Broca's aphasia and three years after a cerebral lesion presented selective difficulties in the production of written verbal numerals from Arabic numerals, a task in which he showed 45% error rate in the pre-test evaluation. The errors were mainly of a syntactic nature (i.e., 907 ⟶ nine zero seven; 7001 ⟶ seven thousand zero one; 114 ⟶ one hundred ten four). The rehabilitation programme consisted in teaching the patient a set of rules that permit the transcoding of the Arabic forms into written verbal ones. The training was divided into five levels of increasing difficulty, in terms of both syntactic and lexical complexity of the trained items and number of facilitation procedures employed (e.g., coloured cues, presentation of vocabulary panels). The programme began with the teaching of the transcoding of two-digit numbers by asking the subject to transcode the left digit by a ten name and the right digit by a unit name. For the three-digit number sequence a rule explicitly stated that the leftmost digit had to be transcoded by a "unit name plus the word hundred" and so on. The completion of all levels required 25 sessions of 30 to 60 minutes each. The patient's performance improved significantly in a post-test evaluation and a follow-up 7 months thereafter indicated long-term effects of the treatment (45%, 0%, and 6% error rate in pre-test, post-test, and follow-up evaluation, respectively).

The second patient, a 25-year-old man, began the treatment 1 year after onset and was assigned to a similar training programme where the transcoding task under consideration was the writing of Arabic numerals from alphabetic forms. In particular, the patient learned to decompose the alphabetic stimulus into constituents and to map these onto the corresponding Arabic forms (e.g., soixante dix [sixty-ten] $\longrightarrow$ 70)[4]. Again, the programme included three levels of increasing difficulty, and several facilitation procedures were introduced to guide the patient in the learning process. The therapy took 17 sessions of 30 to 60 minutes each. The training effects were significant and stable (29%, 2%, and 0% error rate in pre-test, post-test, and follow-up evaluation, respectively).

Besides the different transcoding tasks that were the object of remediation, the two therapies were framed according to the same general principles. The programmes included a strict sequence of highly specific exercises, each of which was targeted to a single transcoding rule or sub-rule. Exceptions were always introduced after the general rule. The ordered progression of the programmes ensured that the exercise requirements were never beyond what had already been taught and, indeed, a 90% correct performance was the criterion to proceed to the next exercise.

The efficacy of this method was proved by the outcome of the interventions. In both cases, the training effects were not item-specific but task-specific, though improvements on different untreated transcoding abilities were also observed. These latter were attributed to common components of the trained and untrained tasks (e.g., same alphabetic input system in alphabetic to Arabic transcoding and alphabetic to dots transcoding) but also to a general *deblocking* effect that may be related to the exposure of the patients to numerical stimuli throughout the training.

In a later case study, Deloche and colleagues (1992) directly compared two different training techniques for grammaticality judgements of verbal numerals. This task consisted in judging whether a written sequence of verbal number lexical primitives constituted a well-formed verbal numeral or not (e.g., soixante vingt [sixty-twenty], is an illegal form in French, whereas soixante dix [sixty-ten], is legal). The patient taking part in the study showed multiple deficits in number-processing tasks, reflecting impairment at the level of both the verbal comprehension and the verbal production systems. The training focused on the syntactic component of the verbal number comprehension system and the grammaticality judgement task was the specific object of remediation. The patient was administered two distinct therapies in succession: the first one simply required him to accept or reject as legal or illegal sequences of written verbal lexical primitives ($N = 616$), and he received feedback on his accuracy; the second one consisted in an explicit teaching procedure of the lexical categorisation of number primitives and of their combinatorial rules for making the judgements. Once again, the teaching programme relied on facilitation cues and proceeded from simple training on the lexical categorisation to more complex training on the lexicosyntactic acceptance/rejection rules and exceptions. The complete training programme included multiple levels and each

---

[4] These transcoding rules have to be adapted to the specificities of the numeral system of the patient's language. In Deloche et al.'s study some rules were specifically framed to take into account some peculiarities of the French numeral system, and especially the complex tens such as "eighty", literally in French "four-twenty" or seventy $\longrightarrow$ sixty-ten" and ninety $\longrightarrow$ "four-twenty-ten"!

level comprised multiple steps focused on specific tasks and items. The results may be summarised as follows: both therapies induced significant improvements in grammaticality judgements; learning the lexicosyntactic rules explicitly allowed a better generalisation of the training effect to undrilled items and, at the same time, training a variety of items was more advantageous than repeating the same few items. In other words, both therapies led to an improvement although their effects were different: covert training induced more item-specific effects whereas overt training induced more rule-specific effects. Interestingly, the treatment on the syntactic component of the verbal number comprehension system gave rise to an improvement not only in other tasks involving this specific component (e.g., magnitude comparison of verbal numerals) but also in tasks such as transcoding Arabic numerals into verbal numerals. These unexpected intertasks transfer effects were interpreted as favouring a non-modular view of the number-processing system as suggested by Campbell and Clark (1988). However, the fact that two distinct therapies were administered in a fixed order to the same patient may have introduced some confounding effects.

Another example of theory-driven intervention is offered by the case study reported by Sullivan, Macaruso, and Sokol (1996). The authors attempted the rehabilitation of transcoding abilities in a developmental dyscalculic 13-year-old boy. A complete assessment of the patient's number processing and calculation skills indicated a deficit in transcoding tasks, more pronounced when the production of Arabic numerals was required. The model of reference (McCloskey, Sokol, & Goodman, 1986) postulated that transcoding of verbal numerals into Arabic numerals requires, besides comprehension mechanisms, the generation of a semantic representation and the translation of this latter into a syntactic frame to be filled with the corresponding quantity represented by the Arabic digits. Given the patient's preserved comprehension of numerical stimuli (as demonstrated by his performance in magnitude comparison tasks) and the occurrence of frequent syntactic mistakes (e.g., *twenty-three thousand forty* $\longrightarrow$ 23,40), the syntactic processes required in the production of Arabic numerals were identified as the functional locus of the impairment. The training programme, comprising two 45-minute sessions, consisted of first, providing the patient with a syntactic frame (e.g., H – T – O for hundred – tens – ones) in order to transcode a written verbal numeral (e.g., six hundred eighty seven) into the corresponding Arabic numeral (e.g., 687), and second teaching him how to generate the syntactic frame by himself in the context of written-verbal to Arabic numerals transcoding. The sets of stimuli presented in the training were of increasing complexity and errors were immediately corrected.

The post-training evaluation indicated an improvement in performance, which was still significant in a 6-month post-training follow-up. The improvement was characterised by a decline in the occurrence of both syntactic and lexical errors, as well as better performance extended only to other tasks sharing the same Arabic numeral production component (e.g., spoken numerals to Arabic numerals transcoding).

Finally, in another study, Jacquemin and colleagues (1991) used the same reconstructive rationale in the case of a early demented patient presenting significant difficulties in the reading of Arabic numerals (for example 279 was read as two thousand nine; see Noël and Seron, 1993, for a detailed presentation of the case). The patient showed difficulty in the reading of Arabic numerals that resulted in an incorrect representation of the corresponding quantities. For example, in a magnitude comparison task of two Arabic numerals, if she read 281 as *two thousand eight hundred one* and 1306 correctly, then she considered that 281 was bigger than 1306. Her deficit was especially disturbing when doing her shopping. Given that the patient had no problem in the reading of one-digit and two-digit numerals, the therapies mainly consisted in using her preserved abilities to read verbal numerals in order to reconstruct her reading of the Arabic one. In a first step of the therapy she was asked to evaluate the number of digits in numerals of various lengths. When she was able to count the number of digits in a numeral (up to six), she was first trained to read numerals three to six digits long with the assistance of a written frame. For example, when she was confronted with a three-digit Arabic numeral she had to put it inside a three-positions frame containing in the right place the word "hundred", and if she was confronted with a four-digit Arabic numeral, she had to use a four-positions frame containing the words "thousand" and "hundred" in the right places. She was then asked to read the whole numeral by taking advantage of the frame (see Figure 2). Progressively the written assistance was faded and the patient had to read numerals of different lengths without any assistance. At the end of the treatment she was also trained to read ticket prices. Thirteen sessions were necessary for the whole training with a level of 92% of correct reading. No information is provided concerning a follow-up evaluation.

Overall, in most of these studies the pretherapeutic evaluation of the patient's difficulties disclosed multiple deficits in numerical skills. Yet the rehabilitation programmes were focused only on one task and the controlled design of the intervention allowed evaluation of the specific and general effects of the training as well as the validity of the functional models adopted as a framework for the rehabilitation

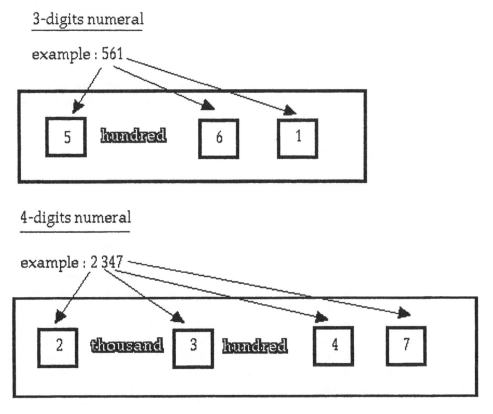

Figure 2.   Example of the written assistance frame used by Jacquemin et al., 1991.

programmes. Moreover, the reviewed evidence suggests that the same principles that provide the basis for designing a rehabilitation programme for an acquired deficit may be extended to the remediation of developmental disturbances. However, only future rehabilitation studies of acquired and developmental numerical disorders may provide clear-cut evidence in favour of this conclusion.

Studies devoted to the rehabilitation of the transcoding processes in the numerical domain have up to now been essentially reconstructive. The reasons for adopting such a perspective are many, but the most important is probably the fact that the amount of knowledge (data and procedures) to be acquired is intrinsically limited given that verbal and Arabic numerals represent restricted domain-specific knowledge. There are indeed only 10 different Arabic numerals, and more or less 20 to 30 verbal numerals (according to the language); and in both codes the syntactical or combinatorial rules are few. The adoption of a reconstructive perspective does not seem an unrealistic objective. At a theoretical level, the fact that Sullivan and colleagues had elaborated a reconstructive programme on the basis of a semantic model, while in the other studies the treatment was scheduled from an asemantic perspective, cannot be used as arguments for or against one or other transcoding model as, in the case of the Sullivan et al. therapy, the deficit was not semantic and the treatment focused on the syntactical aspect of the production of Arabic numerals. However, it would be interesting in future research to evaluate the relevance of introducing exercises of a semantic nature in a transcoding rehabilitation programme, i.e., to compare asemantic to semantic rehabilitation programmes. In the semantic programme the rationale would require two distinct steps: first the subject is asked to transcode a numeral into an analogic quantity (for example by using token of chips of different values), and second, he or she is asked to transform these quantities into the expected output code. Further studies are also required to evaluate more appropriately the respective virtue of explicit teaching of vocabulary and rules, and of programmes using implicit learning procedures with on-line corrective feedback. Furthermore, given the specificity of the domain and the transparency of its level of complexity, transcoding tasks are good candidates for the application of vanishing cue methods that have proved their efficacy with patients with severe memory disorders.

REHABILITATION OF CALCULATION SKILLS

Calculation is a complex and multi-componential skill. Besides numbers comprehension and production mechanisms required for decoding the elements of the calculation (e.g., factors of the problem, arithmetical signs) and producing the solution, calculation-specific processes are called into play. These include (a) knowledge of arithmetical facts, i.e., calculation problems whose solution is directly retrieved from memory (e.g., 5×4); (b) knowledge of arithmetical procedures, i.e., algorithms required to solve multi-digit calculation (e.g., carrying and borrowing procedures); (c) conceptual knowledge, i.e., understanding of the principles underlying both facts and procedures (e.g., the order of the operands in a multiplication problem is irrelevant because of the commutative law). The fact that efficient and skilled calculation requires the interplay of these components does not imply that all individuals master these skills to the same extent. For example, if multiplication tables may be considered "facts" for virtually all educated people, it has been shown that the amount of memorised and automatised calculations may differ greatly among different people (Lefevre et al., 1996). Similarly, even if the understanding of the principles underlying a solution algorithm enables a flexible and effective use of it, nonetheless its accurate execution does not imply any conceptual understanding (e.g.,

Resnick 1982). Thus, it would be improper to assume that conceptual understanding is a well-defined and universal competence among educated individuals. In other words, interindividual differences in calculation skills are even greater than in other cognitive abilities. Pre-morbid mathematical competence varies widely across individuals due to different educational backgrounds and professional activities. For someone whose former job specifically required the manipulation of numbers, for example accountants or traders, the impact of a calculation impairment may be particularly dramatic. These factors have to be taken into account when planning a rehabilitative intervention, given their effect on the patient's motivation and expectations.

In principle, patients may show highly selective deficits (e.g., isolated deficit in multiplication tables) but frequently this is not the case and difficulties are of a multiple nature. In this case, the rehabilitation programme should be targeted first to the more simple and fundamental skills (e.g., simple addition and subtraction) and later on to the more complex tasks (e.g., multi-digit calculation). For example, if a patient's deficit in arithmetical facts extends to all operations, addition and subtraction should be trained first, given that the re-acquisition of multiplication tables may be facilitated by the use of back-up strategies based on the former (e.g., $5 \times 3 = 5 + 5 + 5$).

In order to propose an adequate intervention it is crucial not only to assess carefully the patient's functional deficit, but also to evaluate his/her residual abilities (e.g., What arithmetical problems are still preserved? Does the patient count efficiently? Is the patient still able to comprehend numerals in the different codes as well as the arithmetic symbols?). In all likelihood, this will constitute the basis for designing a targeted therapy.

Rehabilitation of arithmetical facts

Whatever the interindividual variability, simple arithmetical knowledge is essential in numerous everyday situations and the lack of it may greatly affect any individual's quality of life regardless of educational and professional differences. Partially for this reason, attempts to rehabilitate patients with deficits in simple arithmetic have been relatively frequent compared to other calculation impairments. However, some of these studies were only incidentally reported in order to validate specific theoretical issues (e.g., Are multiplication problems with 0's operands solved via a general rule? Sokol & McCloskey, 1990) and they are uninformative about remediation (McCloskey, Aliminosa, & Sokol, 1991).

A more systematic description of simple arithmetic remediation has been provided by Miceli and Capasso (1991). They reported the outcome of a rehabilitative intervention with three patients who showed specific difficulties in the retrieval of arithmetical facts. The patients differed in the severity of their deficit—pre-treatment error rates were 10%, 22%, and 43% for LG, DB, and AM respectively. Moreover, their difficulties varied across different operations. LG's performance was impaired in addition and subtraction problems and to a lesser extent in simple multiplication, whereas multiplication was the most compromised operation in DB and AM. The patients underwent similar remediation programmes: in twice-weekly training sessions over 2 (DB) and 3 (LG, AM) months, the patients were presented with problems of increasing difficulty. At the beginning of the treatment, operations were presented in blocks, whereas at a later stage, addition, subtraction, and multiplication were presented in mixed order. Problems were visually presented and at the same time read aloud by the therapist. Patients were simply requested to answer them in writing or orally. In none of these cases was information about the errors produced or any method of correcting them provided. However, a post-treatment evaluation indicated that for all patients a significant improvement in performance emerged. Moreover, follow-up evaluations indicated that the improvement, although not stable over time, was long-lasting.

A more controlled design was adopted by Hittmair-Delazer, Semenza, and Denes (1994) in the remediation study carried out with BE, an acalculic patient with a highly selective deficit in simple multiplication and division problems. This patient retained only part of his multiplication tables (e.g., 2-times table, ties) but he could still calculate the solution for any given problem by applying back-up strategies based on arithmetical principles (e.g., $9 \times 4 = 9 \times 2 + 9 \times 2$). Though accurate, this method was time-consuming and BE underwent a targeted remediation programme aimed at his reacquisition of multiplication facts. All problems he could no longer retrieve from memory were divided into two sets, trained in different periods in order to control for the specificity of the effects. Training was performed under time pressure although guessing was discouraged. Errors were immediately corrected and the problem repeated. After only 4 weeks BE's performance improved significantly both in terms of speed and error rate. Moreover, the training effects were specific for the problems concerned, suggesting separate memory representation for single problems and even for complements (e.g., 3×4 and 4×3 may be independently represented). More critically for the aims of the rehabilitation study, BE efficiently applied the relearned multiplication tables when confronted with complex written calculation as well as with division problems.

A similar approach was applied in two remediation studies carried out by Girelli and colleagues (1996). Both patients, TL and ZA, were in clinically stable conditions with non-fluent aphasia. As is often the case, although they had undergone speech therapy for some years, their calculation disorders had never been treated before. The intervention aimed at teaching the multiplication tables, which both patients had almost completely lost (pre-treatment error rates were 91% and 81% in TL and ZA respectively). The training scheme followed an AB1AB2A cross-over design, where A consisted of the baseline evaluation and B consisted of the training periods. All multiplication tables (from 2×2 to 9×9) were divided into two sets (pre-treatment performance did not differ in the two sets) presented in separate training periods. This allowed evaluation of the extent to which training effects were of a general or specific nature. The sets differed for the two patients: for TL the two sets were balanced for structural features (e.g., problem size); for ZA one set included 3- and 5-times tables and the other concerned all the remaining problems (in order to minimise transfer of learning effect between the sets).

Training consisted of the visual presentation of the problem, read aloud by the therapist at the same time. Patients were allowed to answer as they wished (verbally while pointing at the same time at the number on a table or in written form). Errors were always immediately corrected and discussed with the patient whenever requested. The training took 8 weeks, with two training sessions per week.

Both patients improved considerably during the training periods (in both patients the overall error rate dropped below 10%), and the effects mainly concerned the respective training sets. However, to a lesser extent, a general improvement was observed, possibly determined by the activation of preserved processes as well as by patients' increasing motivation and self-confidence as the training went on. Interestingly, in both patients, as the error rate decreased over the course of training, the nature of the errors changed dramatically. In TL this modification consisted of the systematic replacement of less plausible errors with more plausible ones: namely from non-table errors (i.e., numbers not included in the time-tables; e.g., $2 \times 9 = 44$) to operand errors close in distance to the solution (i.e., multiple of one of the two operands; e.g., $6 \times 3 = 21$). In ZA, non-table errors and omissions disappeared while a conspicuous proportion of close-miss errors (i.e., numbers close in magnitude to the correct product) emerged. Surprisingly, most of these errors were non-table numbers, as for example, $5 \times 6 = 31$. This remarkable qualitative difference was interpreted as the result of the specific back-up strategies adopted by TL and ZA. TL mainly relied on recitation of the table from $N \times 1$ forward until she could access the solution to the target problem, thus facilitating the occurrence of operand errors. ZA used to work out the solution by repeated additions of the second operand (e.g., $4 \times 5 = 5 + 5 + 5 + 5 = 20$). While he seldom failed to add the required number of operands, occasionally he made calculation errors in the addition itself resulting in close-miss errors.

Both quantitative and qualitative changes in the performance were thought to reflect the building-up or the re-organisation of a semantic network where the associations between problems and answers become more and more specific. Back-up strategies certainly played an important role, as repeatedly postulated for the acquisition of simple arithmetic during development (e.g., Siegler, 1988). A follow-up evaluation showed long-lasting effects for both patients but also the spontaneous use of the relearned multiplication facts in new contexts, as for example in the solution of simple divisions they could not retrieve from memory and in easy text problems requiring multiplication.

Recently a further attempt to rehabilitate a patient with a selective deficit in arithmetic fact knowledge has been reported by Whetstone (1998). The patient, MC, a 42-year-old computer programmer, developed a highly selective impairment in the retrieval of multiplication facts following the surgical removal of a brain tumour in the left parietal lobe. The pretraining evaluation of MC's multiplication facts, carried out on 10 consecutive sessions, indicated an overall error rate of 23%, although the performance improved spontaneously over the testing sessions. The deficit was indeed limited to 18 of 36 unique multiplication problems (once complements are collapsed) showing an average error rate of 42% and the occurrence of mainly operand and table errors.

The unknown facts were divided in three blocks, equated for difficulty and frequency of the single operand. Each block was assigned to one of the three different formats (i.e., spoken verbal, written verbal, and Arabic format) for retraining. MC underwent 12 weekly sessions consisting in study–test opportunities where he was instructed to learn the problems but discouraged from repeating them out loud. The post-training evaluation indicated significant and stable improvement in the retrieval of multiplication tables (97% correct). As for the error rate, there was no format effect, i.e. the patient was equally accurate when he answered problems presented in the format used in training or in one of the two other formats. On the other hand, the reaction time data revealed a match effect: MC answered problems more quickly when they were tested in the same format in which they had been trained. Finally, complements were answered equally fast, despite only one of the operand orders being trained (e.g., 3×7 and not 7×3).

Overall, all these studies produced significant and enduring improvement in the retrieval of arithmetical facts. Simple arithmetical knowledge seems sensitive to practice, even when patients are in a chronic stage and the severity of their deficit is far from being negligible (e.g., TL and ZA). Thus, controlled remediation studies should be promoted whenever the patient's clinical condition and motivation are favourable.

The results so far reported seem to indicate the importance of minimising the opportunity to make errors during training, as repeated errors may create and strengthen wrong associations between problems and answers. The use of back-up strategies is critical and may greatly facilitate the re-acquisition process, as long as these procedures are economical and not error-prone. The teaching of efficient compensatory strategies may indeed constitute the very first stage of a remediation intervention, especially when arithmetical facts are severely compromised. Patients may benefit from being explicitly reminded of the principles underlying simple arithmetic and of their strategic use. For example, the order-irrelevant principle in multiplication reduces 5×4 and 4×5 to a single problem to be remembered, and, although some patients use this knowledge spontaneously to compensate for impaired fact retrieval (e.g., Sokol, McCloskey, & Cohen, 1989), others need external aid. Decomposition strategies may also be taught to simplify harder problems, as for example showing that any $N \times 9$ (or $9 \times N$) is simply $(N \times 10) - N$ or that 7×4 is equal to $7 \times 2 + 7 \times 2$. The underlying principle is to let the patient use known facts to figure out unknown facts. Indeed, learning to put the different facts in relation may facilitate the organisation of this knowledge in memory and consequently the ability to recall it when needed.

Rehabilitation of arithmetical procedures

The knowledge of arithmetical procedures consists of the algorithms required to solve multi-digit calculations. Empirical evidence suggests that individual operation procedures are independently represented in long-term memory (e.g., Lampl et al., 1994); thus it is not unlikely that a patient retains the algorithm for one operation (e.g., complex subtraction) while no longer being able to solve a different operation (e.g., complex addition). The solution of a multi-digit calculation is a complex task. Indeed, the correct algorithm not only has to be retrieved from memory, but also executed via sequential planning, temporary storage of intermediate results, and monitoring (Semenza, Miceli, & Girelli, 1997). In principle, difficulties may arise in any of these stages, each requiring specific targeted intervention. The qualitative analysis of the errors may be very informative for identifying the functional level of the deficit. For example, when errors are systematic (e.g., in a multi-digit subtraction problem, the patient systematically subtracts the smaller digit from the larger one regardless of their location in the top or bottom numbers), they may stem from mistaken or missing knowledge of the required procedure (Girelli & Delazer, 1996). In this case, explanation of the single steps constituting the correct algorithm is essential before any practice may start. Verbalising aloud the steps to follow may help the patient to keep track of the procedural stages. Moreover, visual cues may be very useful for reminding the patient how to proceed. For example, a small arrow pointing left may be written over the operation to indicate to proceed left to right. Similarly, intermediate results may be fully written in order to detect more easily when the carry is required in a complex addition.

On the other hand, the production of highly implausible errors (e.g., the solution of a subtraction is greater than the minuend) might reflect a very poor understanding of the conceptual aspects of calculation itself and might indicate the need to provide this knowledge explicitly. Errors may also be of a complex nature, sometimes reflecting confusion between steps of different procedures (e.g., adding factors in a multiplication problem; forgetting the carry). Miceli and Capasso (1991) have described similar cases. They reported two case-studies where they attempted to rehabilitate a deficit of arithmetical procedures. In both cases, the difficulties in written calculation co-occurred with a deficit in arithmetic fact retrieval, the remediation of which preceded the intervention with arithmetical procedures. The intervention consisted in gradually re-teaching the algorithms for the different operations. At the beginning, addition, subtraction, and multiplication problems were presented separately and the complexity of the problem (i.e., numbers of procedural steps required) was gradually increased over the testing sessions. The patients were encouraged to apply simple strategies, as for example writing down the values to carry over in addition and multiplication, or marking the digits from which the borrow was taken in complex subtraction. A post-treatment evaluation indicated a significant improvement in the performance of both patients, even though neither of them performed at ceiling level.

Acquired deficits in arithmetical procedures are not rare, however attempts to remedy them are scanty. On the one hand, impaired procedural knowledge often co-occurs with poor arithmetical facts and the remediation of the latter may be prioritised. On the other hand, the fact that we deal with complex calculations less frequently, and for most of these we easily rely on the use of the calculator, may have reduced the motivation for a targeted intervention. In principle, however, once basic computational skills are mastered (e.g, arithmetical facts) and the patient is motivated to recover his or her ability to solve multi-digit calculation, a targeted intervention may require a relatively short time to induce significant improvement.

Rehabilitation of arithmetical problem solving

In several everyday situations, we do not just have to carry out a predetermined calculation, but also to infer from the specific context which operation is required and in which precise order it has to be executed. For example, when doing our banking, we may need to check our balance, taking into account that very shortly some bills will be paid (thus a specific amount has to be subtracted) and our salary will be credited (thus a different amount has to be added). In other words, very frequently the calculation itself is only the final step of a more demanding process requiring a careful analysis of the situation, planning, and executive skills.

Current models conceive arithmetical problem solving as a multi-step process that includes the following stages: (1) an encoding stage that leads to the construction of a coherent internal representation of the problem; (2) the selection of an appropriate solution strategy; and (3) the execution of the solution plan (e.g., De Corte & Verschaffel, 1987; Fasotti, 1992; Mayer, 1983; Mayer, Larkin, & Kadane, 1984). Thus, impairment in arithmetical problem solving may arise from difficulties at each of these stages and therefore reflect deficits of various kinds.

It has frequently been reported that frontal lobe damaged patients present major difficulties in arithmetic problem solving, and poor encoding of the given problem has been identified as one of the most crucial causes of their failure (e.g., Christensen, 1975; Fasotti, 1992; Luria, 1966). The possibility of enhancing frontal lobe patients' problem-solving abilities by improving two basic encoding skills—sentence translation and problem-schema understanding—has recently been investigated.

Fasotti et al. (1992) explored to what extent frontal lesioned patients and left-posterior lesioned patients would benefit from a cueing procedure for solving arithmetical text problems. This procedure, originally devised by Mayer (1987), consisted in presenting the patient with a series of multiple-choice questions dealing with sentence comprehension and problem-schema before asking them to solve the problem. The procedure aimed both at helping the patients to build up a coherent internal representation of the problem and at reducing their impulsive behaviour, which was frequently responsible for incomplete processing of the critical problem data. Patients were presented with two series of eight problems of various complexities (i.e., numbers of required operations) in a single session. Only one of the series involved a cueing procedure. As expected, the results indicated that only frontal patients benefit from the cueing procedures, supporting the hypothesis that the difficulties encountered by left-posterior lesioned patients lie in their language comprehension impairment rather than in impulsive behaviour. However, the improvement was short-lasting and patients weré unable to transfer the learning effect to a re-test session, only 2 days after the first one.

Although these results seem to support the inability of frontal lobe patients to generalise positive learning effects (e.g., Lhermitte, Derouesné, & Signoret, 1972; Milner, 1982), we may question whether they would be able to do so when sufficient practice is provided. This hypothesis was directly investigated by Delazer et al. (1998) in a rehabilitation study with three young patients in a chronic stage after a severe head trauma. A cueing procedure was again adopted for the solution of complex word problems (15 problems) of varying complexity (one to five operational steps); patients received 16 training sessions over a period of 8 weeks. Errors produced in answering the questions were always corrected and discussed with the patients.

The training proved to be effective by increasing significantly the overall number of operational steps correctly applied by all three patients in the solution of arithmetical word problem solving. Similarly to Fasotti et al.'s result (1992), these results do not allow us to establish to what extent the cueing procedure improved the encoding process directly or by reducing impulsive behaviour. This latter alternative would be indirectly supported by a delay in the solution process. In the Delazer et al. (1998) study, only two of the three patients were slowed down by the cueing procedure, thus suggesting that the training may affect patients' performance at different levels. Whatever the levels of the effect, a follow-up test (10 weeks post-treatment) indicated that training effects were long-lasting for all patients. Critically, the effects were highly specific to arithmetical problem solving and no other tasks tapping "frontal" functions benefited. Delazer et al. (1998) observed that the training, being targeted to the encoding stage, did increase the number of operational steps correctly solved but had little effect on the execution process, thus leaving unaltered the overall number of problems correctly solved.

Given the encouraging results of these studies, indicating that chronic patients may benefit from specific interventions and also generalise learning effects when sufficiently trained, it seems worthwhile to extend these remediation attempts to other functional components of problem solving, i.e., development and execution of specific solution strategies.

CONCLUSION

The disabling effects of numerical disorders and their clinical frequency leave no doubt as to the importance of developing and promoting rehabilitative intervention for acalculic patients. The rehabilitation of numerical disorders is an extremely recent area of research but certainly deserves concerted effort.

The relevance of a detailed and theoretically driven functional diagnosis is necessary (even if not sufficient; Caramazza, 1989) for designing an adequate rehabilitative intervention. Current models of number processing and calculation provide a much more refined theoretical framework for the evaluation of acquired deficits than in the past. This is a crucial advantage for the development of rehabilitative intervention of numerical disorders.

As already pointed out, very few investigative efforts have so far been directed at this. Nonetheless, these rare attempts were rewarding overall; although a complete recovery was rarely observed, all patients benefited, to differing extents, from the training undertaken and, critically, retained and in some cases spontaneously generalised the training effects. These encouraging results further motivate the development of similar studies aimed at evaluating the feasibility of diverse procedures in calculation rehabilitation.

As far as method is concerned, the therapeutic interventions reviewed here mainly consisted of presenting the patients with numerical and computational tasks similar to the ones used for clinical assessment. However, given the practical relevance of this competence, the remediation may include more ecological tasks as well. For example, acalculic patients frequently have difficulties in handling money, with all the obvious practical limitations that follow. In these cases, the training may include tasks where the patient is required to manipulate real money or tokens of different values for composing a given amount or working out the change. The patients are also frequently concerned with tasks requiring the manipulation of some specific systems such as the division of time into seconds, minutes, hours, days, weeks, and months, and with some specific numerical transformations required in do-it-yourself activities or cooking, where it is frequently necessary to operate some change of proportions, (e.g., a cooking recipe is for four persons and you have to prepare for six guests). It is certainly important to identify more precisely which mathematical procedures and numerical manipulations are required in each of these situations. Consider for example the abilities implied in the daily use of money. In many cases, money exchange requires, as well as knowledge of arithmetical facts and calculation procedures, counting in different bases. For example, if a person buys a bottle of milk priced 36 francs and pays with a bank note of 100 francs, he or she is not faced with the subtraction "$100 - 36 + 64$"! What occurs more frequently is the execution of a series of additions or counting strategies from the correct price up to the given amount. In our example, in giving the change the seller would usually say "thirty seven, thirty eight, thirty nine, forty" while simultaneously handing over four small one-franc coins; then the seller would say "sixty, eighty and one hundred" while adding three twenty-franc coins. Moreover, exchange of money often implies some magnitude-estimation processes. For example, when shopping, one has to monitor the overall cost of the different things added to his/her basket, to compare this approximate sum to the money at hand. In order to pay, then, the person has to select the bank note of the appropriate magnitude (e.g., if the due amount is two hundred francs, it is inadequate to pay with a five thousand franc bank note). Similarly, one often needs to compare products that differ in their prices as well as in their packaging (for example, a one litre bottle of wine and a one and half litre bottle of wine) and, to select the cheapest, one has to transform the prices and perform several proportions. A further important issue concerns the impact of the patient's mathematical deficits on his or her financial and legal matters. In the case of severe mathematical deficits, the patient's responsibility and competence in dealing with financial operations should not be underestimated and targeted intervention may be highly recommended.

It is thus clear that the daily use of numbers implies various and still unspecified type of mathematical knowledge and procedures (e.g., Nunes, Schliemann, & Carraher, 1993; Saxe & Posner, 1983). A better understanding of these competencies is of crucial importance for devising appropriate rehabilitation programmes. Furthermore, the use of ecological tasks and concrete material in the rehabilitation setting may indeed facilitate the generalisation of the training effects to real-life situations, the ultimate purpose of any rehabilitation programme. Finally, as with other cognitive deficits, attention should be directed to the efficacy of using external devices in the rehabilitation training (such as an electronic calculator).

So far, remediation attempts have been concerned with number transcoding deficits and calculation disorders, among which deficits in simple arithmetical knowledge have been the most investigated. However, brain-lesioned patients may present difficulties in many other aspects of numerical abilities, as for example, in manipulating numerical quantities (e.g., Dehaene & Cohen, 1997) or in the conceptual understanding of arithmetic (e.g., Delazer & Benke, 1997). At present, we are not in a position to provide precise directions on how to treat all the different deficits that may potentially be observed in clinical practice, but this must be a priority for future researchers.

REFERENCES

Ashcraft, M.H. (1992). Cognitive arithmetic: A review of data and theory. *Cognition, 44,* 75–106.

Butterworth, B. (1999). *The mathematical brain.* Chatham: Macmillan.

Butterworth, B., Cipolotti, L., & Warrington, E.K. (1995). Short-term memory impairment and arithmetical ability. *Quarterly Journal of Experimental Psychology,* 1(A), 251–262.

Campbell, J.I.D, & Clark, J.M. (1988). An encoding-complex view of cognitive number processing: Comments on McCloskey, Sokol and Goodman (1986). *Journal of Experimental Psychology: General, 177*(2), 204–214.

Caramazza, A. (1989). Cognitive neuropsychology and rehabilitation: An unfulfilled promise? In X. Seron & G. Deloche (Eds.), *Cognitive approach in neuropsychological rehabilitation.* Hillsdale, NJ: Lawrence Erlbaum Associates Inc.

Carlomagno, S., Iavarone, A., Nolfe, G., Bourene, G., Martin, C., & Deloche, G. (1999). Dyscalculia in the early stages of Alzheimer's disease. *Acta Neurologica Scandinavia, 3,* 166–174.

Christensen, A.L. (1975). *Luria's neuropsychological investigation.* New York: Spectrum Publication.

Dahmen, W., Hartje, W., Büssing, A., & Sturm, W. (1982). Disorders of calculation in aphasic patients—spatial and verbal components. *Neuropsychologia, 20,* 145–153.

De Corte, E., & Verschaffel, L. (1987). Using retelling data to study young children's word-problem solving. In J. Sloboda & D. Rogers (Eds.), *Cognitive processing in mathematics* (pp. 42–59). Oxford: Oxford University Press.

Dehaene, S., & Cohen, L. (1997). Cerebral pathways for calculation: Double dissociation between rote verbal and quantitative knowledge of arithmetic. *Cortex, 33,* 219–250.

Delazer, M., & Benke, T. (1997). Arithmetical facts without meaning. *Cortex, 33,* 697–710.

Delazer, M., Bodner, T., & Benke, T. (1998). Rehabilitation of arithmetical text problem solving. *Neuropsychological Rehabilitation, 8,* 401–412.

Delazer, M., Girelli, L., Semenza, C., & Denes, G. (1999). Numerical skills and aphasia. *Journal of the International Neuropsychological Society, 5,* 1–9.

Deloche, G., Ferrand, I., Naud, E., Baeta, E., Vendrell, J., & Claros-Salinas, D. (1992). Differential effects of covert and overt training of the syntactic component of verbal processing and generalisations to other tasks: A single-case study. *Neuropsychological Rehabilitation, 2*(4), 257–281.

Deloche, G., & Seron, X. (1987). Numerical transcoding: A general production model. In G. Deloche & X. Seron (Eds.), *Mathematical disabilities: A cognitive neuropsychological perspective* (pp. 137–170). Hillsdale NJ: Lawrence Erlbaum Associates Inc.

Deloche, G., Seron, X., & Ferrand, I. (1989). Reeducation of number transcoding mechanisms: A procedural approach. In X. Seron & G. Deloche (Eds.), *Cognitive approach in neuropsychological rehabilitation.* Hillsdale, NJ: Lawrence Erlbaum Associates Inc.

Fasotti, L. (1992). *Arithmetical word problem solving after frontal lobe damage. A cognitive neuropsychological approach.* Amsterdam: Swets & Zeitlinger.

Fasotti, L., Bremer, J.J.C.B., & Eling, P.A.T.M. (1992). Influence of improved test encoding on arithmetical word problem solving after frontal lobe damage. *Neuropsychological Rehabilitation, 2,* 3–20.

Girelli, L., & Delazer, M. (1996). Subtraction bugs in an acalculic patient. *Cortex, 32,* 547–555.

Girelli, L., Delazer, M., Semenza, C., & Denes, G. (1996). The representation of arithmetical facts: Evidence from two rehabilitation studies. *Cortex, 32,* 49–66.

Hécaen, H., Angerlergues, R., & Houiller, S. (1961). Les variétés cliniques des acalculies au cours des lésions rétrorolandiques: Approche statistique du problème. *La Revue Neurologique, 105,* 85–103.

Hittmair-Delazer, M., Semenza, C., & Denes, G. (1994). Concepts and facts in calculation. *Brain, 117,* 715–728.

Jackson, M., & Warrington, E.K. (1986). Arithmetic skills in patients with unilateral cerebral lesions. *Cortex*, 22, 611–620.

Jacquemin, A., Calicis, F., Van der Linden, M., Wyns, C., & Noël M.P. (1991). Evaluation et prise en charge des déficits cognitifs dans les états démentiels. In M.P. de Partz, & M. Leclercq (Eds.), *La rééducation neuropsychologique de l'adulte*. Paris: Edition de la Société de Neuropsychologie de Langue Française.

Kosc, L. (1974). Developmental dyscalculia. *Journal of Learning Disabilities*, 7, 159–162.

Lampl, Y., Eschel, Y., Gilad, R., & Sarova-Pinhas, I. (1994). Selective acalculia with sparing of the subtraction process in a patient with left parietotemporal haemorrhage. *Neurology*, 44, 1759–1761.

LeFevre, J., Bisanz, J., Hubbard, K.E., Buffone L., Greenham, S.L., & Sadesky, G.S. (1996). Multiple routes to solution of single-digit multiplication problems. *Journal of Experimental Psychology: General*, 125(3), 284–306.

Lewis, C., Hitch, G., & Walker, P. (1994). The prevalence of specific arithmetic difficulties and specific reading difficulties in 9- to 10-year-old boys and girls. *Journal of Child Psychology and Psychiatry*, 35, 283–292.

Lhermitte, F., Derouesné, J., & Signoret, J.L. (1972). Analyse neuropsychologique du syndrome frontal. *Revue Neurologique*, 127, 415–440.

Luria, A.R. (1966). *Higher cortical function in man*. New York: Basic Books.

Mayer, R.E (1983). *Thinking, problem solving and cognition*. New York: Freeman.

Mayer, R.E. (1987). Learnable aspects of problem solving: Some examples. In D.E. Berger, K. Pezdek, W.O. Banks (Eds.), *Application of cognitive psychology: Problem solving, education and computing*. Hillsdale, NJ: Lawrance Erlbaum Associates Inc.

Mayer, R.E., Larkin, J.H., & Kadane, J. (1984). A cognitive analysis of mathematical problem solving. In R.J. Sternberg (Ed.), *Advances in the psychology of human intelligence*, Vol 2 (pp. 231–273). Hillsdale, NJ: Lawrence Erlbaum.

McCloskey, M. (1992). Cognitive mechanisms in numerical processing: Evidence from acquired dyscalculia. *Cognition*, 44, 107–157.

McCloskey, M., Aliminosa, D., & Sokol, S.M. (1991). Facts, rules and procedures in normal calculation: Evidence from multiple single-patient studies of impaired arithmetic fact retrieval. *Brain and Cognition*, 17, 154–203.

Miceli, G., & Capasso, R. (1991). *I disturbi del calcolo. Diagnosi e riabilitazione*. Milano: Masson.

Miceli, G., Capasso, R., & Temussi, M. (1987). Riabilitazione cognitiva dei disturbi del sistema dei numeri e del calcolo. *Archivio di Neurologia, Psicologia e Psichiatria*, 48, 260–285.

Milner, B. (1982). Some cognitive effects of frontal lobe lesions in man. *Philosophical Transactions of the Royal Society of London, B298*, 211–226.

Noël, M.P., & Seron, X. (1993). Arabic number reading deficit: A single case study. When 236 is read (2306) and judged superior to 1258. *Cognitive Neuropsychology*, 10(4), 317–339.

Nunes, T., Schliemann, A.D., & Carraher, D.W. (1993). *Street mathematics and school mathematics*. Cambridge: Cambridge University Press.

Pesenti, M., & Séron, X. (2000). *Neuropsychologie des troubles du calcul et du traitment des nombres*. Marseille: Edition Solal.

Resnick, L. (1982). Syntax and semantics in learning to subtract, In T. Carpenter, J. Moser, & T. Romberg (Eds.), *Addition and subtraction: A cognitive perspective* (pp. 136–155). Hillsdale, NJ: Lawrence Erlbaum Associates Inc.

Rossor, M.N., Warrington, E.K., & Cipolotti, L. (1995). The isolation of calculation skills. *Journal of Neurology*, 242, 78–81.

Saxe, G.B., & Posner, J.K. (1983). The development of numerical cognition: Cross-cultural perspectives. In H.P. Ginsburg (Ed.), *The development of mathematical thinking* (pp. 291–317). New York: Academic Press.

Semenza, C., Miceli, L., & Girelli, L. (1997). A deficit for arithmetical procedures: Lack of knowledge or lack of monitoring? *Cortex*, 33, 483–498.

Siegler, R.S. (1988). Strategy choice procedures and the development of multiplication skill. *Journal of Experimental Psychology: General*, 117, 258–275.

Sokol, S.M., & McCloskey, M. (1990). *Representing nothing: Neuropsychological evidence*. TENNET Conference: May, Montreal Quebec.

Sokol, S.M., & McCloskey, M. (1991). Cognitive mechanisms in calculation. In R. Sternbeger & P.A. Frensch (Eds.), *Complex problem solving: Principles and mechanisms*. (pp. 85–116). Hillsdale, NJ: Lawrence Erlbaum Associates Inc.

Sokol, S.M., McCloskey, M., & Cohen, N.J. (1989). Cognitive representation of arithmetical knowledge:

Evidence from acquired dyscalculia. In A.F. Bennet & M.McCloskey (Eds.) *Cognition in individual and social contexts*. Amsterdam: Elsevier.

Sullivan, K.S., Macaruso, P., & Sokol, S.M. (1996). Remediation of Arabic numeral processing in a case of development dyscalculia. *Neuropsychological Rehabilitation, 6*(1), 27–53.

Thioux, M., Pillon, A., Samson, D., de Partz, M.P., Noël, M.P., & Seron, X. (1998). A case of severe anomia sparing numerals and ordered series. *Neurocase, 4*, 371–389.

Whestone, T. (1998). The representation of arithmetic facts in memory: Results from retraining a brain-damaged patient. *Brain and Cognition, 36*, 290–309.

APHASIOLOGY

EDITOR

CHRIS CODE
Department of Psychology, Washington Singer Laboratories, Exeter University, Perry Road, Exeter EX4 4QG, UK. Tel: +44 (0)1392 264626. Fax: +44 (0)1392 264623. Email: c.f.s.code@exeter.ac.uk

ROBERT MARSHALL: *North American Editor*
Department of Communicative Disorders, University of Rhode Island, 2 Butterfield Road, Suite 1, Kingston, RI 02881, USA. Tel: +1 (0)401 874 2384. Fax: +1 (0)401 874 4404.
Email: rcmarsh@uriacc.uri.edu

ROELIEN BASTIAANSE: *Book Review Editor*
Faculteit Der Letteren, Rijksuniversiteit Groningen, PO Box 716, 9700 Groningen, The Netherlands.

ASSOCIATE EDITORS

Sally Byng, City University, London, UK
Lise Menn, University of Colorado, Boulder, CO, USA
Xavier Seron, University of Louvain, Louvain-la-Neuve, Belgium
Claus W. Wallesch, University of Magdeburg, Magdeburg, Germany
Robert T. Wertz, VA Medical Center, Nashville, TN, USA

EDITORIAL BOARD

Marcelo L. Berthier, Hospital Universitario, Malaga, Spain
Leo Blomert, Maastricht University, The Netherlands
Hugh W. Buckingham, Louisana State University, Baton Rouge, LA, USA
Jason W. Brown, New York University Medical Center, NY, USA
Stefano F. Cappa, Clinica Neurologica dell'Università di Brescia, Italy
Patrick Doyle, Aphasia Rehabilitation & Research Lab, Philadelphia, USA
Susan Edwards, University of Reading, Reading, UK
Alison Ferguson, University of Newcastle, NSW, Australia
Elaine Funnell, Royal Holloway College, London, UK
Guido Gainotti, Università Cattolica del Sacro Cuore, Rome, Italy
Manfred Herrmann, Magdeburg University, Germany
Argye Hillis, Johns Hopkins University, Baltimore, MD, USA
John Hodges, University of Cambridge, Addenbrooke's Hospital, Cambridge, UK
Audrey L. Holland, University of Arizona, Tucson, AZ, USA
David Howard, University of Newcastle, Newcastle-upon-Tyne, UK
Richard C. Katz, Carl T. Hayden Medical Center, Phoenix, AZ, USA
Herman Kolk, Nijmegen University, The Netherlands, Holland
Matti Laine, Åbo Akademi University, Åbo, Finland
Malcolm R. McNeil, University of Pittsburgh, PA, USA
Skye McDonald, University of New South Wales, Australia
Nina Simmons Mackie, Southeastern Louisiana University, Slidell, LA, USA
John Marshall, University of Oxford, Oxford, UK
Dave Müller, University College Suffolk, UK
Bruce E. Murdoch, University of Queensland, Brisbane, Australia
Jean Luc Nespoulous, Université de Toulouse le Mirail, Toulouse, France
Maria Pachalska, Cracow Rehabilitation Center, Kraków, Poland
Claire Penn, University of Witwatersrand, South Africa
Brian Petheram, Frenchay Hospital, Bristol, UK
Robert S, Pierce, Kent State University, OH, USA
Leonard L. LaPointe, Florida State University, Tallahassee, FL, USA
Friedmann Pulvermüller, University of Konstanz, Germany
Don Robin, San Diego State University, CA, USA
Avraham Schweiger, City University of New York, New York, USA
Leanne Togher, University of Sydney, NSW, Australia
Connie Tompkins, University of Pittsburgh, PA, USA
Klaus Willmes, Abt. Neurologie der Medizinischen Fakultat, Aachen, Germany
Richard Wise, Hammersmith Hospital, London, UK

Founding Editors: Chris Code and Dave J. Müller

APHASIOLOGY is covered by the following abstracting and indexing services: *BLLDB (Bibliography of Linguistic Literature), Current Contents: Clinical Medicine, EMBASE/Excerpta Medica, Linguistic and Language Behavior Abstracts, Medical Documentation Service, Neuroscience Citation Index, PsychInfo, Research Alert, SciSearch, UnCover.*

Submitting a paper to APHASIOLOGY

Aphasiology is concerned with all aspects of language impairment and related disorders resulting from brain damage. Submissions are encouraged on theoretical, empirical and clinical topics from any disciplinary perspective, and submissions which involve cross disciplinary study are particularly welcome. *Aphasiology* will publish experimental and clinical research papers, reviews, theoretical notes, comments and critiques. Research reports can be group studies, single-case studies or surveys, on psychological, linguistic, medical and social aspects of aphasia. Submissions and ideas for the Review Articles and the Forum are welcome and interdisciplinary peer commentary is encouraged.

Abstracts.

A structured abstract of 50–200 words should follow the opening page on a separate sheet, please use the following headings: Introduction (to include background, hypotheses etc), Methods (to include subjects, methods, design etc), Results (main findings), and Conclusions.

Papers for consideration should be sent to an Editor, address given below. Please send an original and three photocopies.

Papers are accepted for consideration on condition that you will accept and warrant the following conditions:

1. You will transfer copyright to Psychology Press Ltd, should the work be accepted for publication.

2. The work is your original work, and cannot be construed as plagiarising any other published work.

3. You own the copyright in the work.

4. You are empowered by your fellow author(s) to make a submission to this journal, and to make any agreement relating to the work.

5. Your work has not previously been published in the English language.

6. Your work is not under consideration for publication elsewhere, in any form.

7. You have secured the necessary permission in writing from the appropriate authorities for the reproduction in your work of any text, illustration, or other material which is reproduced or derived from a copyrighted source.

8. You have agreed with your fellow author(s) the order of names for publication of the work.

9. You warrant that the work does not include content that is abusive, defamatory, libellous, obscene, fraudulent, or in violation of applicable laws.

If it is found acceptable for publication, you shall retain the right to use the substance of the above work in future works, on condition that you acknowledge its prior publication in the journal, and to the publishers Psychology Press Ltd.

The copyright in the work shall revert to you if the paper is not published.

There are no page charges in *Aphasiology*.

Fifty complimentary offprints of the article and a complimentary copy of the issue in which your article appears will be sent to the principal or sole author of articles; book reviewers will be sent three copies of the issue free of charge. Larger quantities of offprints may be ordered at a special discount price. An order form will accompany the proof.

Submissions and books for, or offers to, review should be sent to an Editor, address given below.

Editors

Chris Code, Department of Psychology, Washington Singer Laboratories, Exeter University, Perry Road, Exeter EX4 4QG, UK. Tel: +44 (0)1392 264626. Fax: +44 (0)1392 264623. e-mail: c.f.s.code@exeter.ac.uk

Robert Marshall, *North American Editor*, Department of Communicative Disorders, University of Rhode Island, 2 Butterfield Road, Suite 1, Kingston, RI 02881, USA. Tel: +1 (0)401 874 2384. Fax: +1 (0)401 874 4404. e-mail: rcmarsh@uriacc.uri.edu

Roelien Bastiaanse, *Book Review Editor*, Faculteit der Letteren, Rijksuniversiteit Groningen, PO Box 716, 9700 Groningen, The Netherlands.

Style Guides

Please refer to the following website for the journal style guide, and for more information on our other journals and books: http://www.psypress.co.uk

For Product Safety Concerns and Information please contact our EU representative GPSR@taylorandfrancis.com Taylor & Francis Verlag GmbH, Kaufingerstraße 24, 80331 München, Germany

T - #0190 - 270225 - C0 - 244/170/5 - PB - 9781841699172 - Gloss Lamination